Within the Broken Minds

A Literary Anthology of Fear

Edited by Brittany McMunn and J.C. Flynt
Coordinated by Abigail Wild

Wild Ink Publishing LLC
wild-ink-publishing.com

Editors: Brittany McMunn, J.C. Flynt, Deb Lerew, and Arlene Schwartz
Design and Layout: Abigail Wild

Dear Reader,

In this anthology you will find a wonderful series of storytelling. Our writers are in high school, but some are already published authors and for others this is their first publication. From sci-fi to psychological thriller to the everyday, our authors explore the circumstances that cause fear and the emotions and actions that can come from it.

We have enjoyed watching them challenge themselves and grow from this project. We know that this is only the beginning for each of them and are excited to be part of it.

Please join us on this journey of thoughtful creativity.

Happy Reading,
J.C. Flynt-Wamble
Editor
Wild Ink Publishing

Table of Contents

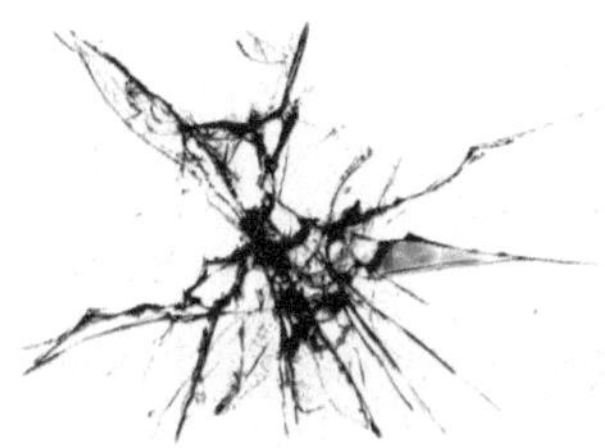

The Waiting Room
by Gracie Lockey

Sirens can be heard from inside the room.

Time ticks by like wet paint drying.

Tick.

Tock.

Tick.

Tock.

Blood stains my white t-shirt.

My leather jacket sits next to me.

Get up.

Sit down.

Get up.

Sit down.

It happens like clockwork.

Will he be, okay?

Will any of us be, okay?

Tick.

Tock.

Tick.

Tock.

Mothers called in because their teenage sons were tex-ting and driving.

Brothers waiting to hear if their sisters will be okay after almost dying in a fire.

Husbands needing to know if their wives are alive after their plane crashed.

Children still too young, too naïve, to know what's go-ing on with their fathers.

Get up.

Sit down.

Get up.

Sit down.

But this time it's different.

This time I'm called in.

He didn't make it.

Nor did she.

But neither will I by the end of the night.

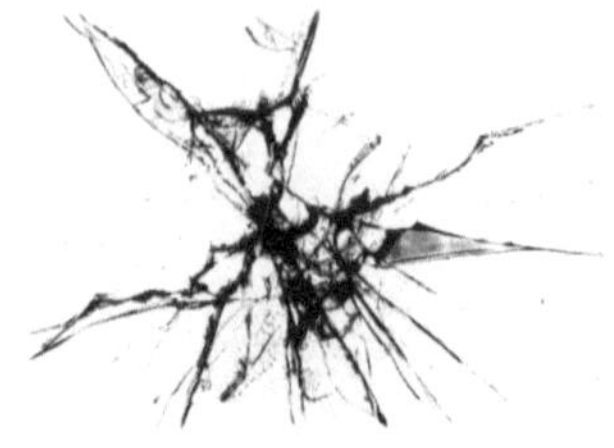

The Sea
by Gracie Lockey

Waves come and go.

Rolling in with the tide.

Rolling out with the current.

With every thought.

With every comment.

With every whisper.

The waves don't ever stop.

There's no break in the white caps.

Nothing but saltwater in old wounds.

And this sea wants me to drown.

Pull me under in its beauty.

Suffocate me until I can't breathe.

Until all I can think about is its water that keeps pull-ing me deeper.

And deeper.

But then I see arms.

A final lifeline.

Trying to pull me out of the waves.

Trying to stop the white caps.

Trying to make the strong current dissipate.

If only I would open to them.

To share the dark secrets that this sea holds.

But when I go to speak.

To tell him the sea's dark secrets.

Not a murmur comes out.

Only an, "I'm fine".

And the arms stay.

Until I am ready to be pulled out of the enraged sea

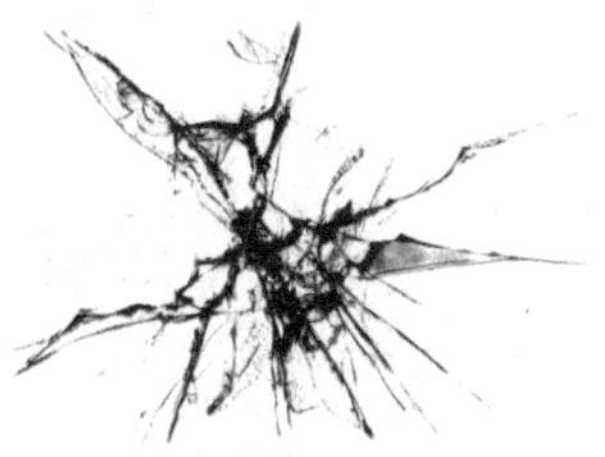

Fear
by Logan Farmer

Riverland was always quiet. That was until scientists unearthed a fossil of what they thought to be a dinosaur. They were proven wrong when it started growing skin again. For months the creature was studied and surveilled. One day it started moving. Within a week, it was strong enough to break out. Soon Channel Five News was covering the story of the escaped beast. Most people had enough common sense to leave town, but those who stayed most likely just didn't have enough money to just pack up and leave. The town of Riverland never experienced tragedy; when they did, it was just a minor occurrence such as a fire. Even that only burned down the abandoned house on Seventh Street. This is the story of the son of a rich CEO named Bennet, the son of a psychic who worked in retail named Ezra, the orphan who lived on the bench in Sharrie Park named Madeline, the daughter of a neurosurgeon named Selene, and finally, the boy who spent his entire life hustling to make enough money to help his mom with rent named Bailey. The tragic events led to one Friday night in a diner. Little did they know their lives would never be the same again.

***

"Bailey! I'm headed to work. I left some money for pizza on the table for you!" Mom called from the living room of our two-bedroom apartment.

"Okay, I love you, Ma!" I called back, slipping on my shoes.

She yelled a quick 'I love you too' and left for work. I went to the kitchen and made some toast and eggs. After I finished my food, I grabbed my skateboard and backpack.

School was fairly normal, besides the fight between Kenny and Lucy. Even that was starting to be a normal thing.

After school, I quickly raced home, threw my backpack on my bed, took the fastest shower in my entire life, and put on my work uniform of a black shirt with the diner's logo and some blue jeans. I skated to work as fast as I could, knowing I was already ten minutes late.

"Hey slacker," Maya said as I walked through the doors. "You best clock in quickly and get started. Rush hour is about to hit, and Veronica's already pissed today."

I clocked in and immediately started cleaning tables and taking orders. Veronica was a sweet woman, but when she was frustrated, you just didn't question her. As soon as four-thirty hit, teenagers filled the place. Maya had four tables, and I had six. Veronica covered the other four. Even though I had more tables, Maya still managed to get more tips. She was a twenty-two-year-old brunette with green eyes and two children, so people either felt bad for her or were trying to flirt with her.

I, on the other hand, did not look as good as her. I'm a skinny boy with bleached blonde hair, hazel eyes, and skin as pale as a ghost. Okay, maybe that's a little bit of an exaggeration, but still. My hair was fluffy and thick, so at least I had that going for me.

"Aye, Bro, come 'ere" I heard someone say. I chose to ignore it, assuming he wasn't talking to me. "Blondie!" he yelled.

He was definitely talking to me. I walked up to their table calmly and spoke.

"How may I help you, sir?" I asked as politely as I could.

"I've been here for four hours, and not once have I seen you stop moving for more than five seconds. Sit." He gestured to the seat across from him.

"Oh, no. I really can't. I have to work— "

He quickly cut me off. "I'll give you five hundred dollars to sit down for ten minutes and eat something." I couldn't refuse that kind of money, plus rush hour just ended, and most people had left. So, against my better judgment, I sat next to one of his friends, I assumed. "What's your name?" he asked.

"Uh, Bailey" I hesitantly replied.

He just smiled, stuffing a fry in his mouth. He then started introducing his friends to me. His name was Bennet, the guy next to me was Luck, and the guy next to Bennet was Kal. After my small break, I stood up.

"It was nice meeting you Ben, and you guys as well" I smiled. As I started walking away, Ben grabbed my wrist. Both his friends let out an "ooohhh." I flinched.

"You're forgetting something," he said, slapping a wad of cash into my hand.

"No, I couldn't take— "he cut me off, shushing me, and went back to talking with his friends.

I just decided to walk away and keep working. A few hours later, a girl with black hair and grey eyes walked in with a boy with ginger hair and icy blue eyes. They sat down, and as I was about to go take their order; I heard people yelling outside. I rushed out and saw two fully grown men kicking someone in the ribs.

"Hey!" I yelled running over to them.

They were twice my size and could definitely take me out, at least they seemed to think so. When they charged at me in one swift movement, I grabbed one of their wrists and put my other arm across the man's body. I dislocated his elbow and used my weight to flip him onto the floor. The other guy just ran away. I walked up to the girl and helped her stand.

"Are you alright?" I asked.

"Besides the fact that I just got a few new bruises, yeah. Thanks." She smiled. "I'm Madeline." She stuck out her hand, and I shook it.

"I'm Bailey." I smiled. "Come inside; I'll get you some food. My treat."

She froze. "Oh, no, no! You've done so much for me already." Something was telling me that if I let this girl leave, I'd regret it.

"Please? Plus, we have a first aid kit, so I could clean the cut on your forehead," I explained. Finally, she caved and agreed to come inside. I sat her at one of the booths and grabbed the first aid kit. As I sat down, the lights flickered. "Hmm, that's strange," I said. Then I just shrugged it off. Once I finished patching her up, I asked her what she wanted to eat.

"Uh, hamburger and fries, I guess." I quickly went back to the kitchen and had them make it.

"Okay, I'll be right back." I smiled, setting her food down. I walked over to the two people that had just sat down. "What can I get you?" I asked.

"I'll take a black coffee," the girl said. Her hair was a silvery white. She had eyes like ice and skin the shade of olives.

"I'll have lemonade, please," said the boy with purple hair and green eyes.

"Of course, I'll be right back with those," I said before walking back to the kitchen. When I brought their drinks back, I learned that the boy's name was Ezra. I think I heard him call the girl Selene.

"Here you are." I handed them their drinks. Ezra seemed frozen. Then the power went out. Suddenly, rain poured down.

"Darkness is coming, and there's nothing anyone can do to stop it," he said plainly. Selene grabbed her phone and called someone.

"Ma'am, it's happening," she said; then after a few seconds, she hung up. Madeline had fallen asleep in the booth, and Bennet was still sitting there eating fries like everything was normal. All the staff were trying to get the generator on while I stayed out here to make sure the customers were okay. A woman burst through the front door. She had black hair with bangs in the front, green eyes, and rings on every finger. She immediately ran over to Ezra, looking him in the eyes, muttering something under her breath.

"You three, come and sit," she commanded. Madeline, Bennet, and I were the only people other than staff in the diner, so we all went and sat with her. Madeline was still half asleep, and Bennet was still eating fries. Ezra still looked very dazed. Selene looked like she was in fight-or-flight mode. I was just confused.

"Listen to me very carefully. All five of you are destined for great things. You didn't ask for this, and you'll probably hate this for a long time." The severity in her voice was unmistakable.

"Pardon me, ma'am, but what are you talking about?" Bennet asked.

"The enlightenment is happening. The shell of the egg must be cracked if the yolk is going to be set free." With those last words, she stood up and walked away, her black dress flowing behind her.

"Let's go to my house. We'll be safe there. I can drive us," Bennet said. None of us disagreed. If we wanted to leave, we had to go now before the weather got worse. We all got into his G-wagon, and he started driving.

"Ben, my mom is working at the soup kitchen; we need to go get her." At this point, I wasn't sure if I was asking or telling him.

"We can't; we won't be able to leave once we get there. Text her and tell her that if she opens the metal cabinet in the back of the pantry in the kitchen, she should be able to push the back wall open. There are stairs that lead to a panic room underneath the building.

It can only fit about six people, but she should be okay," he explained.

"How do you know all of this?" I questioned.

"My mom owns that place," he replied. I texted her the information right before my phone died. We pulled up to an old Victorian-style mansion, and Ben parked in the garage. When we walked inside, there was a grand, silver chandelier that illuminated a soft, warm glow around the room. We all walked up the stairs, following Ben to his room, which much to my surprise, was the size of my apartment. Once we all sat down and introduced ourselves, Ben put on a movie.

"Bailey, when all of this is over, tell your ma that she's not a cook at the soup kitchen anymore," Ben said, looking at his phone.

"No, please don't fire her she— "

He very quickly interrupted me. "She's not fired; she's promoted to general manager. I had my mom look her up in the system when we got here, and your mom has logged three times the number of hours of anyone else. Plus, all the staff recommended her for the position anyway. So, since the last general manager resigned, your mom was chosen to fill the position," he explained like it was no big deal. "My mom is going to meet with yours face to face in a few days to talk about it," he added. I didn't know what I was supposed to say, but out of instinct, I jumped up from my seat and hugged him. He looked very surprised.

"Uh, sorry, but seriously, thank you so much. You don't know how bad we needed this," I said, standing there awkwardly.

"Don't mention it, but we should probably go to

sleep soon; it's almost one in the morning," he replied. We all agreed. There were three couches and five of us. I agreed to sleep on the floor. Madeline tried to volunteer, but we decided she deserved a couch after sleeping in a park for so long. Ezra also agreed to sleep on the floor. We made beds on the floor out of blankets, and we all lay in our respective spots. I fell asleep pretty quickly, but unfortunately, I didn't stay asleep. Well, none of us did really, considering the loud banging on all the windows. Ezra was talking to something with a dazed look on his face.

"It is not what one does, but what one will do that determines their fate. I cast you back from which you came, Asmodeus; you have no power over me." At this point he started levitating and speaking another language. He fell back onto the floor, and the banging stopped.

We all rushed to his side. He opened his eyes and sat up. He looked at us and stood up.

"We're dealing with forces much greater than us, and nobody is coming to save us." His tone was serious, and I could tell he was nervous.

"What if your mom called her friends?" Selene suggested.

"I can ask her, but I doubt any of her coven will help us unless she orders them to," he replied. He sent a quick text to his mom, I assumed.

Thankfully, Selene had an extra phone charger with her that she let me use. I knew my mom was fine because ever since I'd charged my phone, she'd been sending me hourly updates. I just texted her that I was okay. None of us could really sleep after the whole unseen forces banging on the window thing. We just stayed up, mostly talking about random things. By the next morning, there were thirteen women standing on the lawn in front of Ben's house.

"Thank you, Mrs. Corneal," Selene said, referring to Ezra's Mom.

"I've already told you to call me Luna. Now, let's get started. First, we'll need someone to go under," she explained.

"What do you mean?" I asked.

"Well, to ensure that the demon is trapped in Limbo, someone needs to lure him there and then trap him. The thirteen witches here will cast a spell to send you all into the astral plane. Then the five of you will lure the demon into Limbo and fashion a prison that'll hold him, but it will be dangerous," Luna warned.

"What do you mean? Also, why do all five of us have to go?" Madeline asked.

"Because you are the guardians of fate. It is written, and it has been for eons to come. In every past life and in every life to come. It is your destiny," she explained. "Only you can build the prison to hold something so powerful".

"Okay, wait, five teenagers who barely know each other are the 'guardians of fate' or whatever? Whatever that's supposed to mean," Bennet scoffed. It seemed like we all had the same question. I mean, what was she talking about?

"Once one of you goes under, the rest of you have to follow, or that person will get lost in the in between," one of the witches said.

Before any of us could say or do anything, we

were pushed into a circle of salt. All the witches started chanting and speaking in tongues. Then Ezra's mom raised her arms, and I felt my body fall, but I was still standing. I looked around, and the other four of my friends were standing next to me. Then we were shot into a cloud of darkness. We were getting thrashed and thrown around. We landed on the ground, and everything looked dull and dead.

None of us knew where we were or what we were supposed to do but judging by the tornado of lightning and rocks with a bunch of screaming coming from it, that probably meant that we had to walk straight into it. We all looked different. And by that, I mean we were literally glowing. Ezra was the first to start walking, and I hesitantly decided to follow. When we were standing about a foot away from the tornado, Ezra and Selene touched it, closing their eyes. They seemed to know exactly what to do.

"The rest of you get over here now; we can't do this alone!" Selene ordered. When all of us were touching it, the tornado dispersed and we walked straight to the center, where it reformed and sucked us into the ground. We were in some sort of cave or something.

"Oh, you five again. Really, do you never learn?"

As soon as I heard that voice, I started to remember past lives. We always ended up here in this cave with the same intentions: to kill a prince of hell. The only problem is in every life we died. That was how it had gone every single time. Eon's worth of lifetimes, and in every one of them we never left this cave. I froze. Anything I would've said either disappeared from my brain or got stuck in the back of my throat. I was paralyzed by my own fear. The only other time this happened was freshman year when – you know what? That doesn't matter. The point is it hasn't happened in two years.

"Bailey, it's okay. Breathe," I heard Bennet say.

I wanted to say something back, but I couldn't. I wanted to tell him I was okay. I felt a pounding pressure on my head. It felt like fire was coursing down my spine. At that moment, I realized that this was a battle of wills. This was not my fear; it was his. The prince of hell was scared, and I knew exactly what I had to do. I had to fight like hell because if I didn't, I'd die, and so would my friends.

"Give me your hands," I said with a weak voice. We all joined hands, and I immediately felt stronger.

"Oh, what are you going to do? Destroy me with the power of love?" Beelzebub said sarcastically, rolling his eyes.

"No, but you seem to forget that we are the guardians of fate, and even though we failed before, we will not fail again. My whole life, I've done nothing but fear the world. Not anymore, because now I know what I'm going to do with my life: Protect fate from evil like you" I bellowed.

"That's cute." He smirked, waving his hand, and I was thrown into the wall. Then onto the ceiling. Then again onto the floor. None of us stood a chance. We all got beaten so badly most of us couldn't stand. It was our time to give up. It was the only choice we had. Ezra walked over to me and placed his hand on my head.

"You'll be okay. This isn't the end yet; just let go."

He smiled, so I let go. That was it. I was gone. At least I was supposed to be. It took a while, but eventually

I could bring myself back again. If my physical body had died, I wouldn't have been able to, but I wasn't in my body, so all I had to do was rest. Of course, we didn't know that at the time. When I woke up, my friends had left. I couldn't blame them for not wanting to die; plus, they had my body for the funeral, so they didn't know what to do.

"Hey, you failed to kill me, you idiot," I said, standing up.

"What, how?!" Beelzebub screamed. I walked out to the entrance of the cave and used my energy to slowly drain his life force. That was the end; he was finally dead. It was nothing grand, but it was the end. I pulled myself back to my body and woke up.

"Oh, my God, you're alive!" my mom cheered, engulfing me in a big hug.

-one month later-

At this point, my mom started making enough at the soup kitchen. Our friend group has never been closer, and some of us even got into relationships, but that's a story for another time.

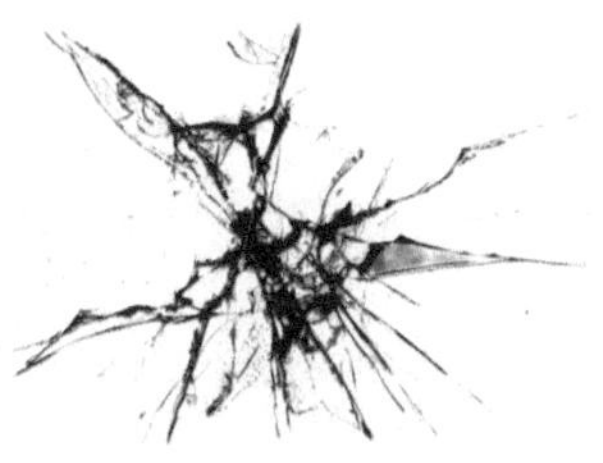

The House with the Lime Green Door
by Sky Corkern

The first time I babysat for them, things were great. If only I didn't go a second time. It was around 7 pm when I walked up to the lime green door of 1313 Rosewood Way. I'd already babysat for them once. The kid was amazing, and the $20 an hour helped with tuition, so why wouldn't I do it again? Before I could knock, Mrs. Pechman opened the door.

"Hello, Maya, I hope you didn't get too lost on the way. Please, come in," she said.

The house was in a heavily wooded area that was hard to navigate if you weren't a local. I almost got lost the first time, but it wasn't too hard to find this place a second time.

Before I could get two steps inside, a small, black-haired boy ran up to me.

"Miss Maya is here!" Bennett hugged onto my leg and jumped up and down, almost knocking me off my balance.

I picked him up and ruffled his hair.

"Sure am! It's good to see you, Little Guy," I cooed.

"I'm not little. I'm dis many." He said, holding up 3 fingers.

I giggled a little and pinched his cheeks.

"We'll be back around 4 am. Is that ok with you?" Mr. Pechman asked, straightening his tie.

"Sounds good to me," I replied.

Mr. Pechman walked out the door and headed for his car, barely sparing me a glance.

"His bedtime is at 9. Here's the money for the pizza. Get whatever kind you want. He'll eat anything."

"Thank you, Ma'am. Enjoy your date."

"Oh yes, before I go, I'd like to talk to you about something." Her tone was hushed, so I ushered Bennett out of the room.

"What's up?" I asked.

"A family in the neighborhood went missing recently, the Johnson's I think they were. I heard they were later found dead in their homes. It's probably nothing to worry about, but don't let anyone in just to be safe," she said.

"Oh god, that's terrible. Thank you for telling me. You make sure to be safe, too."

"We will be," she said before leaving hastily.

I ordered the pizza then played with Bennett and the dog until it arrived. It was about 8:30 when I opened the door to get the coloring book I left in my car when the dog ran out.

"Shit!"

I ran to go get the dog back, praying he hadn't run into the woods. I saw him sitting at the edge of the road, about to dart into the street.

"Charlie! Stop! Fuck!" I screamed.

He sprinted into the road in front of a white pick-up truck. The truck swerved around him, tires screeching as it came to a stop in the middle of the intersection.

I walked up to the car of the speeding asshole who nearly hit the dog and found heavily tinted windows. I knocked on the driver's window and a terrible chill ran down my spine. I turned to check my surroundings, and when I looked back, the window was rolled down.

Inside of the car was sheer darkness. I couldn't see much with the lone streetlight on the road, but I swear it was like looking into a void. I couldn't move. I couldn't breathe. All I could do was look into the empty car.

I still don't think empty was the right word. That implied it could be filled with something. I could only describe it as darkness in its purest form, and it made me want to throw up.

"Miss Maya?" I heard Bennett's voice from behind where I stood, and it snapped me out of my trance to look at the toddler. My eyes widened.

"Bennet, why aren't you in the house?" I asked, raising my voice more than I intended to. The terrible feeling I had earlier was only increasing. We needed to get inside. Now.

I was gonna help you find Charlie," he said as I picked him up and started looking around to find the dog.

"Where's Charlie?" he asked.

"Right here," I mumbled as I grabbed the collar of the dog barking at the car and started running back to the house.

Thud!

I looked up and saw the lime green door that I just hit. It was cracked open, slowly opening more from the force.

I ran inside and slammed the door behind me. I put Bennett and the dog down and locked the door.

"Are you ok, Miss Maya?" Bennet asked.

"Yeah, I…I'm ok," I said. I couldn't stop thinking about the void in that car.

"Ok! Can we watch Aladdin?" he asked.

"Mm-hm, just give me a minute." I took a moment to collect myself and push those memories from my head while I locked all of the doors and windows.

It was 9:46 when the movie finished, so I put Bennet to bed. I sat on the couch and read the book I brought. The same sense of dread I felt earlier never fully going away.

Around 10:30, someone knocked on the door. The sound almost gave me a heart attack at first, but I got up to try and locate the door in the dim light of the single lamp.

The feeling of dread simultaneously worsened then faded as I neared the door. I opened it slowly to find a small boy, no older than 6.

Something about this boy seemed off, and the feeling that had dissipated to the back of my mind worsened. His presence seemed to calm me, but that scared me in and of itself.

"Who are you?" I asked, sounding meeker than I meant to.

"Can you let me in? I need to call my parents," he said.

"I can't let you in. Do you know your parents' number? I can call them for you." I pointed to the landline on the counter.

"Please let me in. It's cold."

My anxiety only grew the more he talked. I could not let this boy inside.

"No, sorry. What's your parents' number?"

"Let me inside…please."

I could've sworn his eyes darkened in color when he uttered the sentence. It sounded more like a demand than a plea.

"This isn't my house. I can't let you inside."

Panic rose in my chest. There was something wrong with this kid. I just knew it.

"Let me in," he said.

His words set off all the alarm bells in my head, and without thinking, I slammed the door in his face and locked it.

"Go away, please," I said from inside.

I got no response, and when I looked outside, he was gone. That helped me to calm down some. I was happy I didn't have to deal with any creepy, possibly possessed, kids.

It was 5:30 am, and I was still reading my book. All the lights on this time as I waited for another update from the parents. Apparently, they weren't going to be home for another few hours.

I heard a knock at the door. I really hoped it was Bennet's parents at the door.

"Who is it?" I yelled.

I didn't bother getting up from the couch. No response. I figured it was just some preteens playing ding-dong ditch or something and went back to reading my book.

About an hour later, another knock.

"Who is it?" I asked, a little louder this time.

"Please let me in. I need to call my parents," a boy's voice said from outside the door.

I don't know why, but I decided to open the door. I wish I knew the reason.

"I told you to go away. Go bother the neighbors if you want, but you're not coming in," I said.

"Let me in," he demanded, his eyes nearly black now.

"Go away, please. Just leave," I pleaded.

"I'm not leaving until you let me in," he said, voice devoid of emotion.

I could barely stand now with my shaking legs, and my breathing became ragged.

"Go away, kid," I ordered, trying to sound less terrified than I was.

I reached for the door handle and started to close it.

"Let me inside," he said.

His darkened irises consumed the whites of his eyes, leaving two holes in the place of them. I froze. It was the same darkness I saw in that car.

"Go away, please go away. P…please," I stammered.

I was on the verge of tears now, body unable to move and head filled with the same consuming sense of dread I had felt many times tonight.

"I want to come inside. Let me in," he said, voice echoing way more than it should.

Finally, I pulled together the strength to shut and lock the door. I wasn't opening it for the rest of the night.

As soon as I sat down on the couch, there was a knock on the door. I stayed silent. Another knock. Then another. Then another. The knocks grew louder and louder, and I put my hands over my ears to try and ignore it.

Then the knocking stopped. Maybe he had given up?

A few minutes later, I heard a knock on the back door. Though it was hard to see through the glass with the reflection, it was easy to make out the silhouette of the small child.

There was another knock. Then another. Then another. I ran to the phone and dialed 911, only for the line to disconnect seconds into the call. I tried calling back, but it wasn't going through.

I sat back down and could feel his empty eyes staring holes into the back of my head when I faced away from him.

There was a knock on the front door, but when I looked back, he was still in the backyard. Another knock came from the front. Another knock from the back. The knocks were loud and fast, making a constant sound.

There was a knock on the kitchen window. Then the curtain-covered windows by the front door. There were knocks on the bedroom windows too.

Every surface on the outside of the house was being hit, the sound echoing in my head. I cried, not knowing what to do. It became unbearable.

"Please! J…just go away! P…please!" I sobbed.

The knocking stopped, and for a minute, it was silent.

"Please! J…just go away! P…please!" I heard from outside of the backdoor. It was my own voice.

I turned to find a tall silhouette standing outside, a figure of the same darkness as his eyes. The same darkness as the car. I felt like if I let it, that darkness would consume me.

I heard my own cries from outside of the front door. Then the windows. Then the knocking came back. It was louder than before. It surrounded me. My cries echoed in my pounding head as I curled up in a ball. I sat there for what felt like hours, the noise never stopping. My body grew numb as my mind grew restless. I needed this to stop. I couldn't take it anymore. It was torture.

As I was about to call out and let him in, everything went silent. The sweet release from pain. Until I heard the lock click and the door start to open.

At this point, my rational mind came back, and I realized, yet again, that I could not let him inside.

"Don't come in! Please!" I screamed, hugging a pillow tightly and burying my face into it.

"Maya? What happened?" I heard Mrs. Pechman yell with worry.

I looked up, and it was really her. She, and her husband behind her, looked startled, understandably so.

I hadn't realized it with my eyes closed, but the sun had begun to rise. By now, it was almost completely risen.

"Maya? Maya!" I heard her yell.

I had missed her coming closer to me.

"I...I'm alright I just..." I was still crying and shaking, seemingly unable to calm down, even with the sense of dread evaporating quickly.

"Take your time. Tell me what happened," she said, steadying her voice.

If I told her the truth, she would think I was crazy. So, instead, I pushed myself up and started walking to the door with shaky legs.

"Maya, tell us what that was about," Mr. Pechman demanded.

"Don't let him in," I murmured.

"Don't let who in?" Mr. Pechman asked as I ran out the door and into my car.

I didn't even bother buckling before I pulled out of the driveway and sped down the street. I saw Mr. and Mrs. Pechman trying to follow me a bit on foot, then giving up.

I didn't look back again until I was home.

***

It's been about two weeks since then, and luckily, nothing else has happened. No more knocks. I wasn't invited back to the Pechman's, understandably. Even if I got an invite, there was no way in hell I would ever go there again.

I sighed, sinking further into the couch, reading a book while the late-night news played in the background. I wasn't listening until a story regarding a particular last name was mentioned.

"In other news, the Pechman family was unfortunately found dead in their homes just last night. The killer is unknown, but police suspect that it's the same person who killed the Johnson family in a similar fashion."

I froze. They must have let him in. I told them not to let him in. The same feeling of dread tried to fill my body, but I pushed it away. I looked at the clock, it was 11:22 pm. I should really get some sleep.

I switched off the TV and lights, laid down in bed, and drifted off to fall asleep.

A knocking on my door woke me. I groaned as I got out of bed and headed to the living room. Who could it be at this hour? As I neared the door, I heard a voice from outside.

"Can you let me in? I need to call my parents."

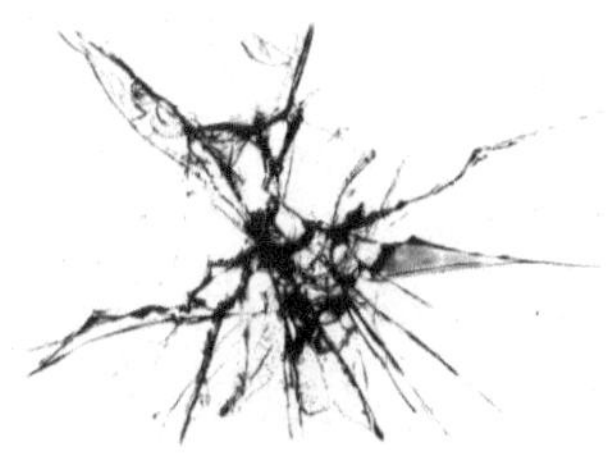

Consumed
by Liam Lamont

May 5, 2024

So much has changed since I last wrote. It's honestly incredible how much life can spiral downward from its greatest moment. One second I'm on top of the world, the next I've hit rock bottom.

Let's see. I unleashed a disease that sent the world into chaos. I got kicked out of the house by my stepmother for the constant attacks I was bringing on the family. And now I'm homeless, on the run, and constantly scared of being scared.

When I won the SeaDeep Contest, I thought it would be the greatest experience of my life. And it was. Until I fucked it up. Bad. How does something like the creature that I brought into the world even exist? Something that lives to destroy with your own fear, kill you from the inside out. They tried to study it before they all got infected, and society dissolved. And it's all my fault, every last bit of it.

And there's Dad. I want to be mad at him for siding with Anne and kicking me out, but I can't. I know it's my fault. I know that I brought this on them. On the world. On myself.

I'm sitting on a park bench as I write this. It's cold. I wasn't ready to leave when they kicked me out. There's some guy with a fear of snakes or spiders or something tearing down the grove of trees in the center of this neighborhood. Not my neighborhood. I couldn't leave the house and then just move the gunmen a few feet from it. That wouldn't be very nice. The man has a chainsaw. The ferocious roar is beating at my skull. I don't know how much longer I can take this. The chainsaw. The world. The fear. It's crazy how much fear can do. Before the disease it was simply a personality quirk; now it's a defining feature. If you have the disease, your fear is intensified by the thousands. You can't function with it existing in the world. For some, it's not so bad. For others, like the man here, it's life changing. He can't function with snakes or spiders or bugs or whatever still in this world. He feels like he has to destroy them all. Like that is the only thing that matters. If he does destroy them, a new fear will take hold, and maybe it will be as bad as this one, or maybe he will be able to find a way to live with it. I doubt it. The disease makes it impossible to live with.

And me? I have the disease. But I don't know what my greatest fear is. And the only way to find out would be to experience it. Once I experience it, I'll never be able to go back. I'll become the man with the chainsaw, unable to function with whatever it is in the world.

So, I have to stay on low ground. Avoid all living creatures. Avoid all smallish spaces. Avoid all storms. Avoid all attractive men. Anything I could possibly be scared of. I just can't experience my fear. If I do, it's over.

May 7, 2024

I was attacked today. I was sitting on the bench, trying not to look at anything, and a group of about twelve people mobbed me. I should really be more careful. I also had a few close calls with fear. As I was running, I almost ducked into a very small alley, and then later I almost ran up a fire escape. Had I done so, and had my fears realized, the results would have been catastrophic. My fear would have been discovered, and my life would be over. Luckily, I caught myself just in time.

I was almost cornered in a side street, but my attackers took a wrong turn and I was able to escape. They found me again in a store that someone with a fear of antiques or something was trying to blow up. I accidentally triggered the explosives, killing five of them and wounding the others. I know they were trying to kill me, but my feelings toward them are the same as those toward Dad. They are trying to kill me for sending the world into chaos, which is very justifiable. I probably shouldn't have blown them up. At least I know I don't have a fear of loud noises.

May 8, 2024

I was attacked again today. I was watching someone burn an entire Walmart's supply of ramen and they snuck up on me. I was able to hide, but still.

I know I said yesterday I needed to find a hiding place, but I never did. I can't think of a place that's not small. If I'm claustrophobic, I'll never be able to enter an enclosed space again. I need some kind of warehouse that's really, really hidden, and even then, they would probably find me. I could always just stay on the run, but the risk of running into my fear is too great. And the risk of being shot. That's a problem too. Maybe I'll just get lucky, and they'll stay away after what happened to that first bunch. But considering I was attacked today, I doubt it.

May 9, 2024

This journal was the only thing I took with me when I left. I've been living off stolen granola bars and bottled water. They are some of the only foods I know I'm not afraid of. I haven't slept in three days, which is good. I may have a fear of dreams, or a nightmare might show the disease what my worst fear is. All I do is sit on this bench between attacks. There's no way forward. No way out. The world is trapped in fear and it's all my fault. And there is no way for it to stop. That's the beauty of it. The fear is endless because it is inside you. There's no cure because the world is in chaos. Pretty much everyone is quarantining or has the disease, and supplies are impossible to reach. I am almost laughing at the impossibility of this situation as I see it on paper. It's absurd. That one little manipulative disease could completely collapse our society. One little mistake. My mistake.

May 11, 2024

I think I need to sleep. It's been almost a week. I haven't been attacked again, which is incredibly lucky, but staying awake for five days straight has to be almost as bad for you as being shot. I don't know if I can though. What if I find my fear in my dreams? That would be the end of everything. My life would be over. It would be impossible to stay away from attackers if I was bent on destroying cockroaches or had to stay outside or couldn't look at anything yellow. Still. It's almost impossible to run with the level of fatigue I have now. It's a Catch-22. I sleep, I find my fear, and I can't run from the attackers. I don't, and I still can't run from attackers. My sole diet of Nature Valley can't be helping either, but at least I haven't found out I have a fear of ramen and joined the guy across the street.

I clearly can't stay on one topic. I need sleep. But I can't get it. Which brings me back to the terrible Catch-22. To sleep or not to sleep, that is the question.

May 12, 2024

I did it. I slept. I realized that I could keep myself from dreaming by waking myself up after about 30 minutes, before REM kicks in, then staying awake for about two hours, then doing it again. I did it about three times, so I should have enough sleep to last me a little while. I'm a genius. No attacks yet. My streak won't last long though.

May 15, 2024

It's been three days since I last wrote and so much has changed. I was attacked by a different group of people today. I always thought their only objective was to kill me, but I guess they're smarter than that. I should have known. I was doing another round of sleeping and they got me just as I woke up. They locked me in a bedroom. Honestly, it's way better than the park bench. It's not small, or particularly dark, there are no bright colors, so I'm good on surroundings. It's the food that's the problem. Every day they give me different food. It's not bad cooking, but if I end up fearing something they give me, everything will be over. My mind would dissolve into chaos, and they would be able to manipulate me without end.

This whole situation just shows how little it takes to go from great to bad, then bad to worse. Just a week ago I had won the SeaDeep trip, now I'm trapped in a bedroom with people who I thought wanted to kill me, but I guess they just want to trap me.

I haven't been let out of this room yet. It's a pretty normal bedroom, aside from the lack of windows. I'm sitting on the bed as I write this. There's a desk that I eat at, a bathroom, a nightstand, your usual stuff. Honestly, I'm content to just stay here. Hopefully that's all they want to do with me. Someone's coming.

May 16, 2024

It went from bad to worse and now to terrible. They read my entire journal. They know how much I don't want to find my fear. I have no doubts that they won't hesitate to use this knowledge. I could see the way they looked at each other as they read it. The two leaders here come personally to check on me every so often. I don't know night from day here without windows. My brain keeps jumping from subject to subject. It's probably a lack of sleep. I don't want to try sleeping here for fear I won't wake up, or what I will find when I do. What they will do to me.

I've been reading back over some of my earlier entries. It's amazing the enthusiasm with which I wrote when I found out that I had won the SeaDeep trip. If only I knew. I taped the letter of confirmation into this journal. "Congratulations, Miranda!" it reads. Congratulations. Whose idea was it to let a fourteen-year-old drive an experimental submarine anyway? I mean, what did they expect? Not this. That's for sure. I don't think I've actually written about the incident, have I? Now's as good a time as any I suppose.

It happened during the SeaDeep trip. It was all going swimmingly (literally) until the driver asked if I wanted to take the controls. We were already near the ocean floor, so I guess he figured there wouldn't be any more of the complex maneuvers that had plagued the descent. He showed me the basics, steering, how to move it lower and higher, that sort of thing, and everything was fine. I stayed on the wheel for about twenty minutes before one of the scientists spotted something. I can't even remember what it was. Some kind of jellyfish, I think. I remember eagerly leaning over to get a good look. Too eagerly. I completely forgot that I was in the driver's seat. The driver shouted at me to turn the sub. I jumped back to the controls. I fumbled for the wheel and jerked it left, directly into the cliff that the driver had been shouting at me to avoid. A small web of cracks appeared in the glass wall of the sub. Water began to seep in. The scientists rushed to patch it, but it was too late. The microbe that carried the fear virus had already gotten inside. Infected me. I can't remember what happened after that. I wonder what the others were thinking. What fears filled their heads? One of them was claustrophobic. As we drove the sub back up, we had to hold him down to prevent him from opening the hatch. I can see now that everyone's worst fears were consuming them. Everyone was being destroyed from the inside out but me. And now my captors know.

I wonder what they will do with their new knowledge. Make my room as scary as possible? Try to find my fear, then torment me till I break? Probably. I doubt they'll keep things the way they are. I wonder what my fear will end up being. It's only a matter of time at this point. Still, I shouldn't think about it. The instant I find out, my life ends. Well, not literally, but my free life ends. The disease will take me over.

Here they come.

May 17, 2024

I was right. They have emptied a room out specifically for finding my fear. They held me down, then brought things in one at a time. Spiders, pictures taken out of jets, needles, anything anyone could possibly be afraid of. And I wasn't afraid of anything. It's amazing. Everything they brought in I was able to look at and smile. No reaction. I now have a way bigger list of things I'm not afraid of. If I had known, things would have been so much easier. I would have been able to climb buildings to escape my pursuers, find a small hiding place, gone to England (well, not really. But if I did, I wouldn't have been scared.) There are so many things I could have done. So many possibilities. Yet, with everything they show me, the list of things I am potentially afraid of gets smaller and smaller, and the chances of finding it get higher and higher. It's only a matter of time. And once I run out, it's over.

May 19, 2024

The day has finally come. It's been two days since they started fear testing me, and there's no way they won't find it today. They've shown me germs, they've shown me snakes, they've shown my clowns, they've shown me whales. If they don't scare me today. . .well, that won't happen.

I've almost come to terms with it. The fact that my conscious life will be over. That I'll be taken over by the disease. Almost come to terms with it. I still don't want to think about it though. I need to squeeze out the last remaining minutes of sane life before I lose it.

This will probably be the final entry in this diary. I should make the most of it. What else is there to say though? One of my captors will probably read this. Fuck you. You have realized my worst fear. Made me find the thing that scares me most. Oh well. Goodbye.

May 20, 2024

They didn't do it. Didn't find my worst fear. They tested everything, and nothing scared me. But I think I know the only thing that can. I know what I fear most, and it was right in front of me this whole time. The disease had me and I didn't even realize. I read over my previous entries before writing this. I was the guy burning the ramen, except instead of destroying my fear, I was avoiding it. I spent weeks without proper sleep, almost got shot to avoid a fear of heights, and restricted myself to food that cannot sustain the human body. Everything that someone with the disease would do, I did. All to avoid fear. That's it. It has been with me all along. That's my worst fear. I'm a phobophobic. The only thing I fear is fear itself. And – if all I'm afraid of is fear – then there is nothing to actually be afraid of. I've endured hours in my captors' fear chamber, and nothing scared me. The only thing they couldn't test was fear, and that's the only thing I'm afraid of. If there is nothing else in the world to be afraid of, then I'm basically invincible to the disease. I've done it. Beaten the unbeatable. Ended this torment. Confronted my fear.

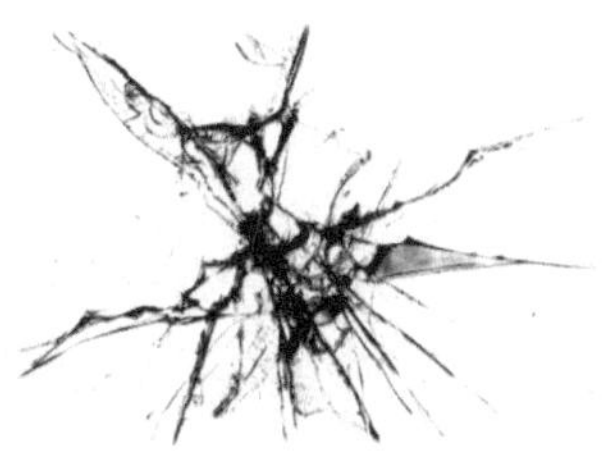

Phobophile
by Sylas B. Polston

On a dirt road I'm standing. Four cops surround me, with their guns pointed at my head. They've "caught" me I suppose.

Four cops surround a man, their guns aimed, poised to fire. The man is short, and round. He wears a white t-shirt which displays an assortment of wild grown mushrooms, and their names. Thick glasses and a tan ball cap complete the look. He seems as if he's a dad that's been taking his family on an RV road trip cross country.

"Hands on your head, now!" A cop yells, and the man immediately obeys.

He speaks with a stutter, mixed with a strong French accent in his voice he's almost unintelligible. "W-w-what is t-t-this about?"

"You are under arrest!" The cop unhooks handcuffs from his belt and walks around behind the man, all while never taking his eyes off him.

"I-I-I don't understand-d? Je parle français! Je parle français!" The man desperately repeats.

The handcuffs snap around his wrists and the cop lifts him up off his knees.

The cop then passes the man off to two other cops who escort him into a cop car. The man cries out as he tries to tell them something, but it is too hard to understand.

***

A cop sits the man down in front of a steel table in an interrogation room. On his end of the table his hands are cuffed around a metal bar. On the opposite side of the room is a mirrored glass.

The cop exits the room without speaking a word, and the man is left in the room alone. He looks around, a look of confusion and nervousness on his face. Several minutes go by before the door swings open and in walks a plain dressed detective and a woman who is his translator. The detective and translator sit down in front of the man.

"What is your name?"

The man hesitates for a second, "C-Claude."

"Last name?"

Claude furrows his brow, unsure of what the detective is asking. The detective looks over to the women. "Quel est ton nom de famille?"

"Oh! Kelley."

"How well can you speak English?"

"A-a little…"

"Can you tell me what you were doing today?"

"I w-was c-collecting mushrooms f-for dinner."
"I see…"
The detective pulls out a headshot f of a girl, with brunette hair, in her late twenties. And sets it down on the table. "Do you know this girl?"

***

Two girls walk through the woods, Claude Kelly is their guide. They smile and laugh as they follow Claude, who points out mushrooms on the forest floor and they pick some and drop them into small foraging baskets. The girl with brunette hair walks up beside Claude, "So where are you from Henry?" Henry smiles, "right here from Virginia, born and raised." He says proudly. "What about you and your friend?"

"We're from Southern California. We've been taking a road trip across the country."

***

"Where are you from Claude?"
"C-Canada, I-I moved h-here a year ago…"
"And you do nature walks, is that correct?"
"Yes."

***

"So how long have you been conducting these walks?"
"Oh, I don't know, almost four years now. This all used to be my parents' land; it was gifted to me after

they died. It's about five hundred acres."

The land had lived within the Walker family for centuries, dating back to the eighteen hundreds, and it had only shrunk in size over time. Now, any fields were almost completely cut out of the property, and it consists of thick wooded areas.

"Do you live on this property still?" the woman asks him.

"Yes. There's a farmhouse only about 500 yards away, in a clearing that I live in."

Henry avoids a small puddle on the forest floor and his foot nearly lands on a worm, but he hops to the side just in time to make sure he doesn't crush the small creature.

"I am sorry my little friend…" Henry thinks to himself. "You can have the dead soon enough. But these wretched lives… they're mine."

***

"N-no, I don't know w-who that is."

"Really? Because she claims that you led her and her friend on a nature walk, and that you aren't Claude Kelley; you are Henry Walker. Is this true?"

"No, it's n-not true. M-my name is C-Claude Kelley, I haven't done a n-nature walk in w-weeks."

A voice comes in from the detective's earpiece. "John, I found a match for this man. He looks like somebody named Joseph O'Brien. A convicted murderer who was set free a decade ago."

"If you really don't know who she is, then why would she have called the cops in a panic? Why were you chasing her?"

***

"If you two want, we can stop in at my house for lunch; it's just in this clearing ahead of us." Henry asks the two ladies with a smile on his face. "There's a nice little outdoor pavilion we can break at."

The two friends look at each other, "that'd be nice Henry, we'd love that." Says the brunette. "Great!" responds Henry.

As Henry walks ahead the brunette's friend tugs at her shirt. "Are you sure about this? We don't even know him." The brunette shrugs, "he seems nice, I trust him."

***

The friend lies dead in the living room. Her body is torn and lacerated from knife wounds. Blood soaks out from beneath her onto the wooden floor. In the next room, the kitchen, Henry holds a pork knife, dripping with blood. He stalks around the side of the kitchen's island. "Where are you?"

He laughs, "I don't wish you any harm…I just want to kill!" He jumps around the corner, holding the pork knife ready to pounce. The brunette girl jumps up, meeting the crazed man's knife with a frying pan. The pan smashes into his hand and glances off, hitting him in the jaw. He collapses to the ground, knocked out.

The girl stands in shock for a moment, still holding the frying pan. After a few seconds she comes to her senses and drops the pan, making a run towards the door of the old house.

Minutes pass before Henry Walker awakes. He sits up, rubbing his jaw. Then he quickly realizes what happened and scrambles back up to his feet. Dazed, he reaches down and grabs the pork knife before chasing after the brunette girl.

Henry reaches the wood line outside of the clearing. He looks down towards the ground, where a sneaker print lies in a small puddle of mud. He follows the print into the woods and tracks after the girl's path.

He traces the path until he reaches a dirt road. He steps onto the road, looking both ways but can't see any sign of the girl.

Just then, obscured by the trees, two cop cars round the corner. Henry immediately throws the pork knife behind his back, where it lands in a cluster of bushes by the wood line.

The cop cars skid to a stop in front of him and four cops jump out, their guns aimed.

***

"We know you did it…Joseph. We found the knife in the woods and your fingerprints are on it. And as we speak there is a squad searching for your house right now. They will find the girl you murdered, and you will go to prison."

"Now tell me, why did you do it?"

Joseph searches around the room, his face twitches. "Why did I do it?" He learns forward, towards the detective. His eyes dark as he smiles. "Because her fear was worth it!"

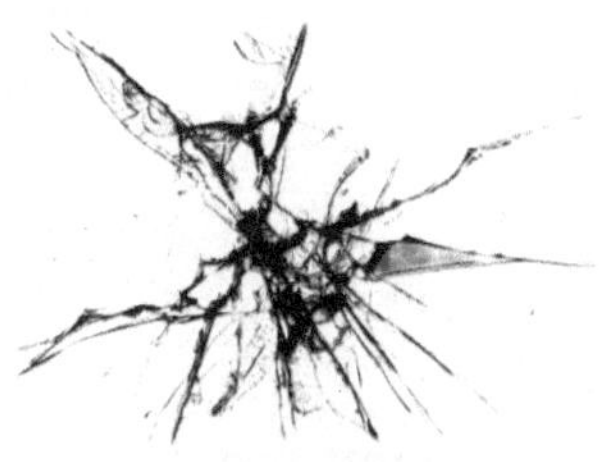

Halloween in Africa
by Elizabeth O. Ogunmodede

Pennsylvania, U.S.A

There was every reason to celebrate, but Levi wasn't buying into Diana's happiness.

Levi was Diana's brother, who was now downing a cup of red rooster smoothie at the breakfast bar. Right outside the window, the midday sun glowed orange. Orange was Diana's favorite color. Levi had been with his sister all afternoon. It was Saturday and Levi often went to soccer practice in the morning, and then he'd drop by his sister's apartment and stay for the rest of the afternoon.

"I've always wanted to explore Africa, Levi. Now is the time." Diana, put two nice slices of fresh Madeira cake on Levi's plate. She had gone to the mall that morning to shop for some groceries.

"You could go on an adventure to China or… or…maybe Dubai, but Africa is just not the place for you. It's dangerous, and I am scared for you." He sighed, stabbing the cake with his fork. "I've often heard that Africa is the world's hottest continent, and it's totally disease-ridden. The tales of conflicts and poverty are just unbearable."

Diana put away the rest of the cake for when her friends might come around. "Well, that's why I'd like to go there and see how people survive, live good lives, and still look beautiful." Diana smiled, ruffling Levi's hair. "You're trying to look out for me lil man, and I appreciate it, but a part of me longs for Africa. And mom is in support of me."

"Does Greg know?"

Greg was Diana's new boyfriend. Levi liked him best, unlike the previous ones. Greg was a manager at the head office of a famous clothing brand. He was posh and cool.

Diana walked over to the freezer and grabbed the chocolate ice cream.

"D'you want some?"

"No." In Levi, Diana saw a reflection of their deceased father. His smile, spirit, and caring ways. "Are you trying to snub my question?"

"I'm not, Gummy Bear. He knows," said Diana.

Levi raised his brow. "And?"

"Gregory is willing to give us a try at long distance. The difference in time zone is sickening, but we'll try FaceTiming and seeing each other over the holidays if it works. Satisfied?"

Levi smiled, pushing his dirty blonde hair away from his face.

"Well, that's a relief. I thought you had broken up with him. You're just so unpredictable, you know."

Diana flicked his forehead. "Duh! You don't have to worry about me. Worry about your grades and getting into college. Janet and Fred are also going with me, which is a good thing. By the way, Louis and Pamela have been there for about three years, and I'll be working with Pamela at our outlet in Nigeria."

Diana reached across to clasp his hands. "All you need to do is to take good care of yourself and mom. I'll be fine, Gummy Bear."

Later in the week, Diana treated Janet and Fredrick to lunch in her apartment.

Janet and Fred had become Diana's best friends at work after Pamela was transferred to Nigeria about four years back.

At that time Diana didn't want to be far away from her dying father, whom she greatly adored. Recently, there was need for foreign expertise in Nigeria, South Africa, and Ghana. Diana had filled in for Nigeria, and she clinched it.

Diana made bacon and eggs, fried potatoes, fried bread doused in tomato ketchup, fried tomatoes, and fried mushrooms for lunch.

Over glasses of fruit wine, they gossiped about work and dreamt of their lives in Africa.

***

For the Halls, October 31 was a time to celebrate.

Diana's dad, Robert Hall, was born on October

31, many years back, and coincidentally, Levi happened to also be born on October 31.

When Diana parked her ride outside their home—a red-bricked cottage with a slated roof—she grabbed her orange shoulder bag and two wrapped-up boxes from the passenger seat.

Dolly, Diana's mom, was having a word with a teenager at the porch. The girl was Levi's lab mate who lived next door. Her name was Eve…or was it, Eva? Diana couldn't remember.

"Hello mom," said Diana, kissing her mother on the cheeks.

The girl smiled at Diana. "Martha Lubov Dracula? I love your costume, Diana."

Diana replied to the teenager and then said to Dolly, "I'll be inside, Mom."

Gregory, Levi, and Diana had come around the day before to set up the house for the Halloween/Levi's party.

When Diana walked in the front door, she couldn't help loving the interior décor.

The house was dimly lit with green and red lights. "This is Halloween" by The Citizens of Halloween was playing through an MP3 device in the sitting room. There was a skeleton bartender in a corner of the living room and dead red roses in different vases. On the walls, hung scary Halloween portraits. Spiderwebs were draped across the room, and there was quite a bunch of flameless black candles placed in jack o'lanterns.

"Hey sis. Happy Halloween," said Levi, emerging from the kitchen dressed like Hawk Moth.

Diana opened her arms and pulled him into a tight hug. "Happy birthday, Gummy Bear."

"Please, keep that name to yourself for the rest of the day. Thanks, anyway." He smiled, collecting his presents. "Two different boxes? That's huge!"

Ever since Levi had turned into a teenager, he didn't like being called Gummy Bear in public, but Diana knew that, secretly, it warmed his insides.

Levi hugged Diana. "Thank you. I think I love you," he whispered into her ears, giggling.

"What am I interrupting?"

Behind them was Gregory, sipping from his glass of black magic Jell-O shots, dressed up like…DRACULA?

Diana placed her hand on her hips and turned to Levi. "You sold me out, traitor! You're unbelievable."

"Well, it was worth a ticket to watch my favorite football player live at the stadium with Greg." Levi pouted, giving his sister the puppy-dog eyes. "Plus, we saw a 3D mystery and crime movie afterwards."

"I need hands in the kitchen, kiddos," said Dolly, walking straight to the kitchen.

Greg winked at Levi, and they fist-pumped.

"I saw that." Diana scoffed, making her way to Dolly as the boys tagged along.

"Hmm! This looks tasty!"

Levi's creepy skull birthday cake, grilled chicken skewers, spider pizzas, mummified apple pies, sauced and finger hot dogs, and many other treats were on display on the kitchen counter and on the island.

Dolly shook her head. "I didn't invite you to come in here and eye-eat the food, Diana. Let's prepare the salad." Dolly took a grater and passed it to Diana, but Gregory was quick to get a hold of it. "You don't have to do this Greg."

Greg smiled politely. "Levi, go set up the table. Babe, slice the cucumbers. Dolly, have a seat, please." He said pulling out a stool.

The rest of the evening was a success with kids and parents from the street coming around later to have much fun.

***

Lagos, Nigeria

Diana Hall and Pamela Ross bonded tightly over the years. Three years in Nigeria together had been a wonder. They lived together, went to work together, and did almost everything together.

Diana toured the most amazing places in Lagos, tasted delicious African dishes, and learned a bit of the Nigerian culture, thanks to Pamela who was always there to pull her through.

The doorbell rang, and Diana left Pamela with setting up the table on the balcony. It had rained the day before, but now it was such a beautiful September afternoon.

At the door were Akachi and Chinara, Africans from the Ibo tribe of Nigeria who worked at the same outlet as Pamela and Diana.

"Hello, Ladies." Diana pulled both women into her embrace as soon as they walked in. She led them past the wallpapered sitting room, through to the airy balcony which overlooked the busy streets of Lagos.

"Hey, Babes," said Pamela with a wave. "Chinara, you look gorgeous!" she cooed.

Chinara twirled around. "You can say that again, Pamela. It was a new arrival at Eril's last week, and it's worth the money."

Diana walked into the balcony with a jar of chilled, fresh orange juice. Akachi sent in some ripe oranges from her garden the day before, upon Diana's request.

"I was thinking that I could go to Eril's to braid my hair this weekend. We could have a girls' hangout at the movies, after that. What do you think?"

The ladies loved the idea.

Pamela poured glasses of orange juice for everyone, and for starters, she dished out chicken pepper soup that she made that morning.

"You should have seen Pamela getting all worked up over Chinara's pepper soup recipe this morning." She scooped a bit of the sauce and gave a comical look. Then, she dug into the chicken, and let out a groan of satisfaction. "I think it's nice."

Pamela gaped. "You call this nice! Diana, give me some credit."

"Fine…fine. I think it's succulent." A chuckle escaped Diana's lips. "I cooked the rice, Guys." She turned to Akachi and Chinara who were seated across Pamela. "You would love it."

Pamela uncorked a bottle. "Who's up for some wine?"

"Is that white wine?" Akachi asked. "I don't take white wine."

Just as Pamela poured some more juice for Akachi, Diana filled her glass with wine. "So, I was wondering if you have an idea of what Halloween is."

Chinara waved her hand around her head dramatically. "That word makes me feel faint. Halloween is literally the devil's holiday."

Diana went into a coughing fit. Immediately, Akachi ran to her side, almost tripping on something, and patted Diana's back. Pamela hurriedly passed a glass of water to Diana.

"Chi…" she gave a mild cough and cleared her throat. "You're ridiculous. Where on Earth did you learn that Halloween is the devil's holiday?"

"It's pretty obvious. Judging from the dark shade of colors that's been used to celebrate the event. Like black, orange, and purple."

Akachi chipped in, "Not to mention the scary costumes. People just love dressing up like villains and ghosts or stuff like that…"

"Yeah, all these are just related to the devil, you know," Chinara concluded and sighed.

Pamela and Diana couldn't help laughing out loud as if on cue.

"Halloween is not what you think, ladies. It's a wonderful fun activity."

When Pamela said this, Diana jumped in, "For me, Halloween is a time to bond with my family and friends and get to put a smile on the faces of kids. For the past two years, I haven't celebrated Halloween. I can see Halloween coming. I feel the energy. It's so strong, and I can't afford to not celebrate it."

Akachi wrapped her braid around her finger and said, "What has this got to do with us?"

***

Cairo, Egypt

Every Sunday, Louis often went bowling with Ra, his Egyptian friend who lived next door with his family and worked at a museum in Cairo.

Today, Louis was sprawled on a sofa in his lounge, eating fluffy buttermilk pancakes because Ra was on duty at work. A war documentary was playing on his TV.

Louis was born to a Louisianan lady and a Parisian father. Growing up in Louisiana with a single mother, all his memories were of America and not of France. He loved American foods and culture.

When Louis' mother divorced his father, she went on to get married to an African man whom Louis liked much more than his biological father. When the opportunity to work in Africa came, he opted for Ghana, his stepfather's homeland, but he found himself in Egypt later.

He took a gulp of lemon juice and made a mental note to drop in at Sameera's house at noon. It was her birthday, and she was throwing a little party at her house. Sameera was a close colleague from work.

He seized his mobile from a side table and answered an incoming call.

"Hi," he said into the phone.

"Hey, Louis. What have you been up to, Man?"

He frowned. "Who's this?"

"Are you kidding me right now? It's me, Diana!"

There was a long pause on the line.

Diana? How many Diana's did he know? There

was Diana Zimmerman from his days back in Louisiana…Diana Hall from…

Louis let out a throaty laugh. "Jesus, Diana! I'm so sorry. I had lost your contact. It's been ages since we spoke."

Munching on the last bit of his pancake, he said. "What's going on? Fred told me that you were in Nigeria, and since then, I just seemed to forget about reaching out to you."

From the other end, Diana rolled her eyes. "There's a lot going on, Man. We need to talk."

***

Pennsylvania, U.S.A

Diana's traveling to Nigeria was pure torture for Levi, he was stuck at home with his mom, went skating occasionally with friends, and sometimes Greg would drop by. But all of these weren't what he wanted. He wanted back his partner in crime, his best friend, his everything.

The week after Diana left, Professor Lancelot who instructed Levi's history classes, taught nothing but prehistoric times, ranging from African times to European times. There was just a whole lot of world history to learn.

By break time, Levi would skip lunch with his friends and sneak to the school library where he would wander around, picking out different books on ancient Egypt.

Miss Sawyer, the librarian, had an eye out for him. She'd come to learn his favorites and would always save a new entry on prehistoric times for him. She even allowed him to leave school with the books.

When Levi woke up on October 26 with a terrible headache, he was unbothered. Why should he be when he stayed up late looking at computer screens while doing thorough research? He read books on prehistoric times with dim lights until midnight to avoid Dolly coming into his room. And he'd often watch any movie he could lay his hands on through the night, so long as it was about ancient Egypt.

It was October 28, and Levi was eating grits with shrimp at the dining table when his mom walked in with a box of tissues. Dolly had just called in at Levi's school to check him out because he had developed flu over the weekend and needed to stay back at home.

"Are you sure you don't want chicken and waffles? There's maple syrup topping to go," Dolly asked. She took a seat across Levi at the table.

"Nah."

Dolly passed a plate of chicken to Levi, and he dug in.

"Diana called yesterday, but you were fast asleep, already."

Levi sneezed, covering his nose with tissue. He felt so sick. He hated flus. "What did she say?" He was happy she called but sad that it took her another week to call again.

Dolly said, "Give her a call. She wants to speak with you."

Greg dropped by in the evening with a new book on Egyptian mummies he had promised Levi the day before, plus, a new movie he knew Levi would love. Dolly was next door at Eve's home because her mother was hosting a get-together for the ladies around the neighborhood.

Greg made hot green tea for Levi and ordered fried catfish with fries and coleslaw. Then, they both snuggled under blankets in the lounge and watched Interview with the Vampire.

Later, when Greg left, Levi called Diana, and on the second ring, she picked up.

"Hey," he said, a bit hesitant. He wanted to tell her how much he missed her and act all babyish, but he gave it a second thought.

"Gummy Bear!" Diana sounded so happy. "I've missed you so much. Mom said you're down with a flu."

Levi sniffed into a tissue. "Yeah. I feel so sick. You know how much I hate flus. I had football practice today, but I couldn't make it. Greg just left." He added, "He reminds me of you."

"Levi…" Diana sighed. "We're throwing a Halloween party in Africa. It's going to be your eighteenth birthday, right? I want you to be here with me, and mom doesn't mind."

"Africa?"

Diana responded, "Well, it's Egypt precisely."

Levi smiled. Maybe the flu wasn't terrible after all.

***

Cairo, Egypt

Louis chatted with an excited Sameera. The truth

remained that no one could help being excited, for it was Halloween.

Louis took a sip of his Halloween punch and darted a quick glance around the room. He felt the exciting thrill course through his body once more. Everyone was wearing a Halloween costume piece or another.

Greg caught up with his friend while Diana was engaged in conversation with Akachi, Chinara, and Femi, a dude from Nigeria who had a weird bag clutched close to his chest. Fred and Pamela were having a chat with Fred's Ghanaian friends. Janet also had a couple of South African friends around. At one end of the room was Levi, he was wearing a nose mask and having a little conversation with Pili, Ra's son, who was doubled over with laughter.

When Diana rang Louis that Sunday, she told him that she was interested in throwing a Halloween party in Lagos, and she wanted to have him around.

Boo! Halloween parties were for kids, Louis thought. He introduced something classic in its stead.

Ra showed up, and Louis immediately recognized his musky eau de parfum. Ra always had such powerful radiance about him.

At once, Diana knew Ra was the perfect tour guide. There was this bright smile on his face that reached his eyes, and he seemed to hold everyone's gazes. Ra was simply everywhere.

He welcomed them and said, "I am happy to lead your batch this afternoon." Maintaining eye contact with Louis and Diana, he grinned. "I believe that we're going to have so much fun. Let's begin the tour from one of our most excellent display rooms."

As they walked along with Ra, people took photographs of every eye-catching artifact they happened to come across.

Ra knew exactly what they wanted in about twenty minutes, a thrilling Halloween moment, and he'd long been guided on what to do.

He led the batch to a display room of different gold grave masks of ancient Egyptian kings. From then onwards, they were led to see different mummies from ancient Egypt.

Not far from Levi was his sister. She looked happy and engrossed in the whole tour stuff. Levi didn't fancy any of the lectures. He knew what Ra intended to say before he even did.

"C'mon, let's go," he whispered, pulling Pili along. There was much more to do.

The tourists were being led through different statues of ancient kings and princes.

"Femi, isn't this lovely?" Chinara was eyeing a life-sized sculpture of a prince which was painted reddish brown. "There's just so many fascinating things about Egypt."

Femi smiled, trying his best to look patient. Each time he tried to make an escape; Chinara was always out to disrupt.

He took a step back. "I have to use to the restroom. I'll be right back."

"Why don't you put this down?" Chinara motioned to his bag. "I'll help keep it safe."

"It's fine right here with me."

Chinara made her way towards him. "I insist Femi. You've been with it all day. Take a break from your burden. What's in it anyway?"

Femi felt his insides boiling. Was she possessed by some negative spirit? "Stop being difficult, Chinara! Please," he snapped.

Walking away, he didn't look back to see the astonished look on Chinara's face.

For Levi and Pili, there had been so many stumbling blocks to overcome.

Now, Pili stood behind Levi. He was tense and weak at the knees. He whispered, "Levi, are you sure about this? It could be true for all we know."

With the back of his hands, Levi cleaned beads of sweat from his brow. He was so not stepping down. He took a deep breath, trying to calm his nerves.

"Argh! Pili, you're making things difficult for me. What possible harm can a fictional book do?"

Pili pinched his nose bridge. His heart was in his mouth. He wished he hadn't offered to help Levi get past security protocols to the book of spells. For the love of God, he was praying and hoping that the book was truly just fiction.

There was a power blackout just as Levi made it to the book. It was placed on a sculpted slab in an enclosure. Almost immediately, "Monster Mash" by Bobby Pickett hit Levi's ears. He hadn't been expecting a Halloween soundtrack.

"Are you okay?" Pili asked. His face was the perfect definition of horrified. "This rarely happens."

Levi pulled out his phone and switched on the flashlight. "I think it's all part of the Halloween drama."

He flipped through the pages of the book. There were no hieroglyphics, and it was the translated version, just as Pili had said. When he found the mummy resurrecting spell, he took a deep shaky breath.

He announced to Pili, "I think I've found it."

As soon as Femi found the perfect room, he unzipped his bag and brought out his father's native gong. He was unsure of when the right time to take the try was. Femi's father, Ifagbemi, a voodoo priest, would be enraged to learn that his native gong was missing, and Femi couldn't place a finger on the punishment to be prepared against. It remained that he couldn't escape his father's wrath.

None of that mattered so long as he could find out if the gong could summon non-Nigerian witches and wizards. The hosts of this tour wanted something classic. What else could be more classic than having a bunch of witches and wizards around to grace the event since this event was all about witches? They had to be honored that he, the son of a great voodoo priest, honored Chinara's invite to this event.

When the lights went out and the blast of music hit his ears, it was now or never. He raised the gong and beat it just the way he had often heard his father do.

In no less than three seconds, witches, and wizards he'd never met before assembled in their different animal forms. They all came along with an aura of light that disappeared as soon as they changed form.

At the center of the room was a large serpent. It transformed into a dreadful looking witch, with eyes as red as the blood of the humans that Femi knew they loved to drink in their coven of witches and wizards. Her red eyes scanned the room in hopes of finding Ifagbemi, whose summon she had recognized.

"Who are you?" her thunderous voice boomed. "You don't toy around with me. You wouldn't live to tell the tale."

Employing gesture magic, she waved a hand at Femi, raised him up from the floor against his will, and slammed him straight into a wall a couple of times, leaving trickles of blood on the wall.

She gave a satisfied throaty laugh and said to the other witches, "When you invite us for no just cause, you invite trouble. Go now, take control of everything!"

Back at the tour room, the lights came back up in a few minutes and everyone seemed to be in pairs, dancing to the music.

"Have you seen Levi? I've tried calling him, but I've been unable to reach out to him," Diana whispered in Greg's ear, slipping her hand away from his grip. "I've got to go find him."

"I'm coming with--" Loud screams from the horde of tourists in the room drowned Greg's voice.

Diana was one of the first people to see the group of scary looking people, all dressed like swamp witches in appalling costumes. They appeared right in the middle of the room like some fallen angels from Heaven.

"What's going on here?" the old woman at the front with a dreadful headdress like Medusa's questioned. Immediately, the music came to an abrupt stop. She was the one who had just sapped Femi's soul.

She gestured her hand at a little kid and sent him floating in the air toward her. "I need an answer!" she screamed into the little boy's face, causing him to burst out in uncontrollable tears. She loved the sound of his cries, to her, they were as lovely as music.

The witch groaned in despair. "I think it's rude that we didn't get a proper invite to this party."

She raised her hand toward the exit and locked the door. There was no such thing as a smile on her withered face.

The witch growled, blowing down great statues and artifacts from the middle of the room. Broken bricks and shards of glass hurled in different directions, hitting anything and anyone in their way. This earned a myriad of screams from everyone.

Just then, there was a loud noise that sounded like loud bangs and screeches. Noises like whimpering and groans followed.

What could be louder than the disaster created by the evil witch? Diana's instincts screamed, Run, but there was nowhere to run to. The evil witch blocked the exit. Diana had to find Levi   as soon as possible.

Well, Levi and Pili were in a big mess. Levi was done chanting the spells and nothing seemed to happen.

He turned to a wide-eyed Pili. "I told you, Pili. This is all fiction."

His laughter was caught up in his throat. Fourteen seconds later, there came a gut-wrenching groan from the next room. Pili was the first to scream. Levi flung the book of spells away and fell to the ground, crawling on his butt as he tried to find his way out of the room.

Upon their exit from the room where the book of spells had been kept, it looked like the security guards in the building had been drugged and dragged to the hallway. There were lifeless-looking bodies here and there, all through the hallway.

"What more could possibly go wrong?" Pili asked, nearly in tears.

From the corner of her eye, Diana caught her brother running into the room from another entry, and he was followed by none other than Pili, Ra's son.

Greg was the first to make a move. He grabbed Levi tightly. "Where have you been Levi? You scared the crap out of your sister."

Levi screamed, "We need to get out of here, now!"

That was all it took for the sound of shattering glass to resound in the building and scarier growls kept coming. It sounded like a multitude groaning in pain. Tears rolled down Pili's cheeks.

Mummies burst through the walls toward them.

A mummy gripped Fred by the neck, and Fred felt his skin crawl. The pungent smell oozing from it made Fred puke. The last thing he heard were everyone's screams as the mummy bit into him, causing a flood of great pain.

As though an order had been given, the others joined in picking their nearest prey to devour.

The witch and her minions shot up at the mummies, pulling the very last bit of powers they could, but the ancient magic from the mummies was superior to that of the witches.

The evil witch chanted some spells as fast as she could, but another mummy was quick to grab her. It let out a mighty groan and gnawed her head, hurling her against an enclosure that broke right away.

Greg called out to Diana, "Get out of here!"

She turned around to find Levi, but Greg was already pulling Levi out of the room, ignoring the seething pain in his left arm. Greg had forcefully hit his left arm against a sculpture amidst the chaos. The fear of dying on foreign soil steered him towards his escape.

How the emergency exit had been activated was what Diana didn't know. She took to her heels immediately, wiping sweat from her face. She was choked as she tried to squeeze past the packed exit. Mummies lurched at the emergency exit, grabbing at prey trying to leave. Fear gripped her heart, and she couldn't stop running for her life.

The last thing Levi saw was Pili's head being chomped off, then, Ra trying to save his son. From behind, another mummy grabbed Ra and dug straight into his face. Tears blurred Levi's vision as he fought to look away.

Later, Diana would stay up all night, crying for all her friends that she lost. She'd often cry for Louis who was on life support and wish that Pamela had survived. There was just one person there to comfort her—Greg. Greg meant the world to her.

Eleven minutes after making it out of the museum, the military arrived with machines that Levi would later learn to be Alien Evacuators which had been built to terminate mummy and alien invasions around the world.

There was so much that Levi wished to correct, but all he could do was to burn his entire archive of ancient Egypt. That didn't stop his frequent nightmares and the fear of mummies. He'd often scream out loud from his dreams, and Dolly would come running into the room, worried for her son.

Those nightmares left him petrified. It seemed like every night, he returned to that scene to witness the death of the innocent over and over again, and the brutal attack of the mummies. He'd always wake up with his clothes drenched, shivering in his mother's arms, and he'd cry himself back to sleep. Whenever he was alone, his instincts would always whisper to him, It was all your fault, Levi. Pili died because of you. Different screams and agonizing voices would keep ringing in his ears.

Levi stopped participating in class. He totally withdrew from family and friends, and he wanted nothing else but to stop existing. If only that would bring back the souls that had been lost.

When Dolly walked Levi into the psychologist's office for therapy, she was at the brink of tears. She missed the cheerful side of her beloved son.

As Levi walked into the white, spotless room, slightly hunched. He pulled off his hood and sat across the kind looking lady, hands clasped on his knee.

He was ready let it all out, the memories, the pain, the fear, and he didn't care one bit if speaking out could put him in trouble.

All he wanted was to be sane again.

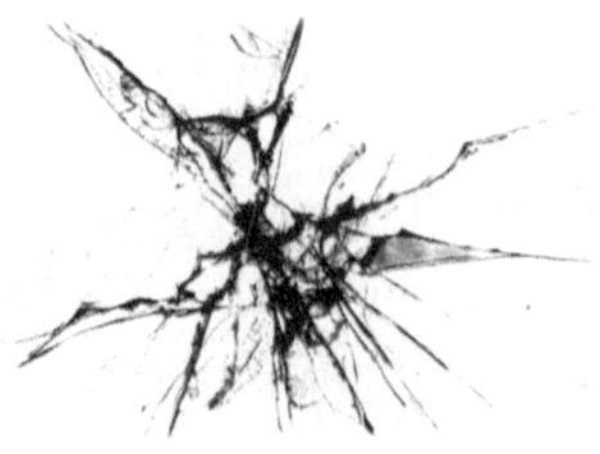

Error: Intermediate
by Wolf S. Helms

Walter tripped and fell perhaps for the fifth time in his terrorized run. He was not weak, for he was a spelunker and archaeologist of some note, as proven by his having been called upon for this particular discovery. However, he was in territory he rarely visited. Normally he was within a ruin, or in a half-finished foundation in the middle of a city examining some small artifact, but at this point he was crashing, or more exactly thrashing, through briers and brush within an East Tennessee valley headed toward one of the many creeks. He had left his meal, car and friends at the top of the rise where a diner sat on a poorly paved, mostly gravel parking lot abutting a five-lane highway.

He had use of only one eye, perhaps the other had been so thoroughly blackened by a baseball bat swing that it had swollen shut or perhaps the jab from a bowie knife may have done more than slice cleanly and completely through the upper portion of his nose.

Earlier:

Something had set the men in the diner off as Walter had entered. He heard one person finishing a sentence including the word, "artifact," before all was silent except for the bubble of oil and the sizzle of bacon upon the grill.

The first swing had been the hack from a man with a bowie knife, who was at the cash register. This blow cut to the bone of Walter's face with a grating vibration shooting pain throughout his head. A moment later the woman behind the counter handed a fat waiter the baseball bat from beneath it. Walter had been struck again long before he could have perceived the effects of the first attack. He had immediately fallen and scrambled under the bench and out the door as a man stepped in with a shotgun. The door's automatic arm had been slow enough to let Walter get out without standing up or touching it.

He had immediately run for their SUV but had promptly been chased as he heard the last screams of his colleagues and friends. He did not have the keys so, if it had been unlocked, he merely would have gotten in to die. He knew where the backup keys were, and he could get out of his situation with the vehicle, but without it he was doomed. He would need to find alternate transportation or find a way to circle back to the SUV.

From there he had ran toward the road, but a truck rolled up in front of him and blew its horn as people with weapons chased behind him. Perhaps the driver was not associated, but Walter did not wait to determine that. He put his years of rock climbing and exercise to use and sprinted westward into the particular situation he was now in.

Walter began to scramble back up the bank somehow breaking through the ordered lines of those hunting him undetected. Yet as he got to the road, someone shouted from below and fire billowed up after him. The flame thrower did not ignite much and its user himself was charging up through the burnt section. Supposedly there was a drought, but Walter did not see any evidence of that in the effects of the flame thrower. He once again reached his friend's SUV, pulled a magnetic plastic box from within the inner side of the rear bumper and jerked the key from it. He was in the vehicle with the engine alight moments before the flame thrower wielding man reached the top of the hill.

As Walter slammed his machine into reverse while pressing the gas a compact pickup truck swung out of a parking spot and blocked his way. Walter barely noticed as the rear window shattered and the opposing vehicle was shunted aside.

Walter put the vehicle into drive and sprayed gravel into the undercarriage of the compact truck as he spun the steering wheel and ripped off someone else's bumper. Fire engulfed the rear end of the SUV but to little avail before the black top roared beneath Walter's wheels. A semitruck loaded with scrap metal belched black smoke as it blocked the road to the west. Walter jerked the wheel as he slammed upon the brake, and the ABS engaged as he turned. When the vehicle's rear end was nearly perpendicular to the road, he hit the gas and the vehicle burned rubber as it completed its turn. Walter let up enough for the vehicle to regain traction before making the SUV work for all it was worth.

An old GMC station wagon pulled out of the diner's parking lot screaming with its excessive throttle in first gear far longer than an automatic transmission would have allowed. The vehicle was gaining ground within a very few seconds in spite of Walter's continually climbing high speed.

Other vehicles joined in, and Walter watched as a school bus exited its normal rounds to park blocking another road and all the eastbound section of the highway leaving an exceedingly small sliver of passage formed by a gas station's paved lot. Walter was forced to nearly stop or plow into a gas pump or the building due to the excessively close layout. He squeezed through and passed in front of the school bus just as its driver was getting it back into motion in an attempt to block him further. Walter's GPS stated, "In twelve miles the destination will be on your left." He determined his course of action. There would almost certainly either be allies ready to aid him in fending off those chasing him or their corpses at his original destination.

Walter hogged the road so that his pursuers could not encircle him and so that he could take tight curves more sharply. After a time, the road became a series of switchbacks. While rounding one, he saw the aforementioned GMC station wagon screaming its way down a steep double rut path which seemed to act as a short cut for the switchbacks though it was obviously of excessive danger. The GMC's driver was attempting to hit him at a thirty-degree angle, use Walter's vehicle to cessate his dangerous direction, whilst forcing Walter off the road and down a cliff. Walter slammed on the brake as the vehicle neared its collision and a moment later the vehicle careened before Walter, yet its driver was expert enough to not go off the side.

Walter was partly encircled and yet the vehicle before him was accelerating and taking turns far faster than Walter dared even in his less than logical state. Shortly after, he slewed around a switch back to face the GMC sitting across the road just before a four-way stop.

The road was somewhat elevated over two sections of grass-covered, rough appearing ground, and Walter had a mere three choices: collide, stop or take the unbeaten path. He chose the latter.

As he came off the raised section, the vehicle's undercarriage sent up sparks and the SUV nearly flipped though somehow it righted itself with a sudden jerk in the power steering that nearly annihilated the meager control he had. Walter regained control and pulled left just before hitting the raised perpendicular road. In the rear-view mirror, he watched as his severed front bumper cover flipped over repeatedly before his machine crashed to the ground with a squeal of tires and a shuddering jolt which nearly eliminated control once more.

Walter slammed the steering wheel back left and held it in the road as he watched the GMC get back into motion with its aforementioned extreme RPM. It was obviously an ungoverned manual with a modified or swapped engine.

The GPS stated, "Your turn will be on the left in one hundred feet." The station wagon was tailgating but Walter chose to apply his brakes anyway. The vehicle kissed his bumper before its driver overcorrected and lost ground as Walter swung left onto what he thought was the right driveway.

When he looked at the GPS's screen, he saw that

he had turned in one driveway too soon and thus he did the logical thing and ran through a barbed wire fence separating the wrong driveway and the other.

The archeological discovery had been made when a sinkhole had engulfed a portion of the driveway the owner was driving on and he said that it was as if a trapdoor had been built there for the explicit purpose of driving a vehicle into it; thus Walter was only partly amazed by the uniformity of the crevasse as he slipped underground. When he looked back, he saw that the GMC had regained its tailgating position.

The GMC's windshield spiderwebbed as someone within began to fire through it. The driver's side broke out before the operator crashed into one of the widening walls as the horsepower got the better of him. Walter saw that the man who had been using the flame thrower was the driver. The man in the passenger seat was the fat one with the baseball bat.

Behind the GMC, a seemingly new Mack semitruck thundered inward with its red paint and chrome offsetting the dull brown, gray and green of the catacombs.

Walter had been distracted from his driving far too long for it felt as if he had struck a staircase or perhaps only one stair for his vehicle dropped down as he looked up to see a piece of stone slide out of his path as if on gimbals.

"Holy shit," breathed Walter, a total realist who feared he had potentially fallen due to strain. As he drove, he saw more pieces of stone moving until a long passage opened perfectly to admit his car. It didn't take long to reach an amphitheater of the catacombs. The front end of the vehicle dropped sickeningly. When the front hit the floor, it dropped a few feet more. The next paving stone was reached, and the car dropped further this time rolling onto its roof due to a previous over-correction. The roof crumpled toward Walter's head as the vehicle again somehow caused the floor to descend under its weight.

As Walter looked up at the opening, the semi screeched to a halt with sparks flying from its side which was pressed to the wall due to the sudden braking and locking of the brakes on one side. The driver began to get out as the semi finally stopped moving at the edge of the first drop which turned out to be a band of steep stairs. Walter unbuckled and rolled onto the ceiling and out of the windshield's vacant location.

Walter looked up at the massive space he was trapped within and saw gear after gear rotating rapidly and continually within the walls. Machines of such presumable antiquity should have been in complete ruins and yet these still clattered endlessly without any sound of friction. The GMC pulled up beside the semi and the man with the flame thrower shouted as he got out, though the shout was overshadowed by a great clunking sound. Walter looked up to see the walls of the passage, which had once seemed to be a part of the hill, slide to crumple the GMC and semi between them. The man with the flame thrower dropped it and took hold of the fat man's hand and began to pull upon him. A thin man could easily have escaped from between the two stones for the vehicles were a good obstruction, but this guy had an immense 'spare tire' and was stuck solidly. Furthermore, it looked as if he were suffocating. Walter held him in contempt. A baseball bat to the eye produces a supreme lack of sympathy. Walter turned, tracing the gears in the roof, until he found himself looking up at an immense gate formed of what appeared to be pure emerald slabs.

No wonder these people wanted no one near their certain riches. If only they could keep the site from the hands of the 'do-gooder' researchers of the more civilized world.

A sound of friction occurred from within the gears and Walter was blinded by a great light as the gears spontaneously stopped spinning. A surge of warm putrid air flooded from the space beyond. When Walter opened his eyes, he saw an opening into a great cavern in which winged humanoids stood. The talons of their wings acted as pincers to put rotten human corpses into their mandibled mouths though they had all been frozen with shock.

Walter didn't scream. He had no air to scream with for it was all applied to the purpose of motion. The flame thrower man jerked his weapon off the ground and pointed it towards the gate as he shouted incoherently over the shrieks of the winged ghouls or night-gaunts.

Walter made his way up the stairs as if he were moving down them instead of up, yet somehow, he was not the target for the assault. He had no clue why they flew only for the man with the flame thrower and his fattened friend. Red light filled the space as the flame thrower pummeled the ghouls back and a tremendous crash arose from the gateway. The view had changed as a series of gears rotated.

The view was of a green sanded beach with black water and that was all Walter was ready to perceive for there was some long-legged thing in that image that he was not prepared to further examine.

Walter reached the upper level and looked back to see that some great dark gray sea monster formed like a crab combined with an octopus had slipped through. The flame thrower man was still spewing forth fire, burning corpse after burning corpse, which fell upon their backs before him.

Walter ran by the wall toward the pair but found an opening and unhesitatingly entered. He feared for his life thanks to the knowledge that the walls could crush him but knowing that a sudden compression was the risk better taken than death by fire or by carrion eating ghouls or furthermore great ugly beasts with tentacles, great tri-clawed hands and crab legs.

There was a great crash of sound as Walter ran, and when he turned, he saw that some portal to another world had opened behind him. From it was emitted a black fog within which there was a muffled voice while flashlights swung around seemingly at random.

Walter turned left and came upon a Mack dump truck which had seen some use. He turned and passed on through another corridor. He came out to see the same flame thrower man with his friend's top half behind him. The man was still fighting the ghouls but in a new location and he had not realized that his friend had been cut in half by whatever portal through which they had fallen.

At the next intersection Walter found himself looking toward a trio of dead ends. Furthermore, there was a man with a rocket launcher looking up at a creature which had come through a silver portal. The creature was hideously designed with a vertically oriented mouth and split face. The jaws opened and the man with the rocket launcher screamed obscenities as he locked his rocket into place and fired with the tube still tucked under his arm, aiming for the blood-soaked mouth within which torn overalls and a plaid shirt could be seen.

The man was immediately trapped between the jaws of the beast though they were not living anymore. Walter saw the flame thrower man's flame thrower along with his severed hand and thus immediately inherited the weapon. A small blue jet came from the muzzle acting as a pilot light and the fuel gauge was at one half of the original charge of the tank placed on the top.

Walter put the flame to good use eliminating a hooved rubbery being with vaguely human features. The silver portal disappeared and became an opening into some snow filled place in which a wooly mammoth ran from a saddled raptor with a rider being some form of tentacled barrel with a peculiarly positioned articulating head.

Walter moved on into a different corridor but after the third step he found himself falling against the wall and he rolled against the roof before falling to what should have always been the floor.

As he got up, he stepped through some portal which produced no visible effect and he found himself within a room somehow lit from the stone floor to show large bear traps. Walter stepped back and heard one of the traps snap shut, but when he looked down, he found that he wasn't the one in the trap. The trap had only closed around the solid wood-like hoof of one of the hooved creatures.

This was when Walter screamed as he plunged forward watching as his foot came down upon a trap, yet it did not close upon it. Instead, his foot vanished before he found himself in an arched moss-covered corridor. He reached a fork and took the right path.

A strong voice shouted, "Delta Squad, Do you know your position?" from ahead. Walter jerked into an opening before turning to his left and putting his flame thrower to use against a group of tentacles. Whoever was calling upon Delta Squad was not there though they had sounded as if they were.

Walter began to sprint across the corridor when a massive tentacle with suckers the size of a car door's window slipped silently toward him as he jumped into a new tunnel just barely escaping his demise. He got back up looking at the floor before him. All was black yet he heard something skittering. Walter lifted the flame thrower to see better with the flame and saw a blanket of black marching toward him. He screamed again as he pulled the trigger spraying the hallway with fire. Tiny bodies crackled and popped within the blaze. Arachnids of a rather extensive size were the culprits; many scorpions and many black widows.

The fire was adequate to rid the tunnel of all but their crisped remains and Walter proceeded ahead. He turned into another hallway and found himself confronted by a hallway of golden bricks. When he turned around, he saw a wall of the same material. Beneath him was grated flooring and he looked through it to see another hall of golden bricks. Walter turned and proceeded down the golden hall hoping that he was out of danger, and he found that he did not step back into another world. He proceeded to climb the stairs of Fort Knox and beat upon the safe door until he noticed a red call button. He fainted immediately after pressing it.

Walter woke in a hospital bed with bandages covering nearly all his face, an IV was within his left arm and furthermore his wrists were cuffed to the bed. He itched and felt heat within his body though there was no pain. His lips were numb and yet he still could tell that they were dry and cracked. When he spoke asking where he was, he was unable to recognize his voice before a purple glove sticking from a white sleeve reached out and turned a valve. Darkness accompanied him down once more until the blackness receded preceded by a sensation which felt as if his heart was pummeling itself into oblivion.

The room had been changed, no window anymore, the walls were of white plastic and the lights were dimmed fluorescents. A man wearing a black suit with a red tie stood at a substantial height. He had a pale coloration, and his hair was in a well combed and precise mess and his eyes were purple rimmed from lack of sleep and closed. When he opened them, their irises were orange and his pupils had white or green reflection.

"I am Lennard Church. You were bitten one hundred and twelve times, more or less, by an unknown species of spider… unknown to everyone except for us and a few other organizations like ours ran by other countries. Were you in Tennessee when strange things began to happen?"

"Yes," Walter's voice had improved, and he realized that his tongue had swollen, "but I burned the spiders."

"You burned the normal spiders which contained the abnormal ones, most of which survived and some of which were small enough to be caught up in the eddies caused by the fire… you probably thought that they were ash and coals when they touched you. Their venom was what put you under.

"We had a team there a short time ago. I am sorry to say, we were forced to stage a terrorist plot in which a highly acidic chemical formula was accidentally released destroying their laboratory and making a long list of dangerous effects within a mile radius. You were in that 'laboratory', and we don't exactly have definitive policies for what that means, so we are flying by the seat of our pants right now."

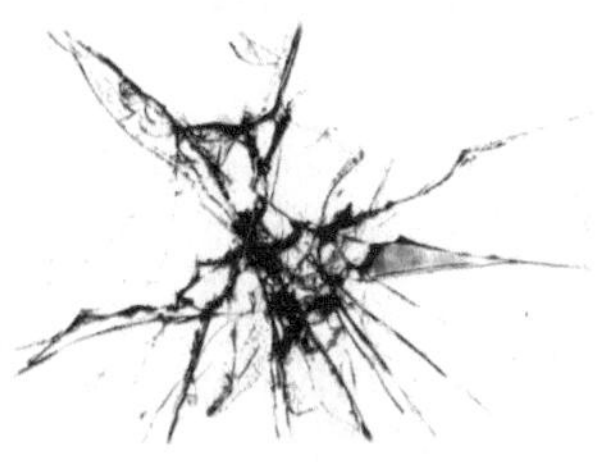

The Unknowable
by Wolf S. Helms

Dominick B. Klinsky of the Russian Heavy Tank Brigade sat within the electrical and engine room of the tank which he kept moving amidst the invasion of the USA, via Alaska, after the recent Nuclear Arms Elimination Treaty freed everyone from the "M.A.D." (Mutually Assured Destruction) ideology. The tank was more of a nuclear naval submarine on tracks than a standard armored vehicle.

A series of dull thumps shivered through the speakers as their microphones detected gunshots and deadened their volume before applying all signals to the speakers. Klinsky examined another of the monitors, the upper machine gunner's nest. There the gunman fired not looking through his gun's sights as various dents appeared, and sparks flew on the opposing side of the armor. "There are too many snipers, I'm coming down." stated the gunman as he stepped down and closed the hatch and began looking from a port made of several inches of ballistic glass within a narrow slot on a different screen.

"We just intercepted a transmission, an evacuation order. We just lost long range radar. Talk to me, tech. What in hell are those? We are losing all tags. All tags are disappearing from our screens. Are there EMPs? Forward command, do you read?"

From within Klinsky's very tank came the reply, "We can read you and all seems to be well." Damn all lines like that and the proficiency of coincidence to apply the counterpoint within the next several seconds as if fate were being provoked unto abnormal actions in a fabled "jinx."

Klinsky saw as the port the gunner was looking out of became a glowing thing of unfathomable brightness as static imprinted itself into the camera's view to extensive degree. The gunner fell back from the port as the screen reconnected with partial static indicating nuclear detonation, in spite of the treaty. The gunner's face was reddened as if sunburned and his eyes were obviously blinded, most likely permanently.

An explosion rocked the tank, and every single screen began to flicker as the nuclear reactor climbed ever so slightly in its controlled criticality. Klinsky watched that screen, the only one without static, with rapt attention prepared to act if something within the reactor went bad, but nothing did - until the next Davey Crockett detonated. He immediately pulled all but two rods from the reactor as he heard the third detonation before a trilogy rapped away and silence reigned momentarily before being split by a second sporadic volley.

America had just stated its preparation to nuke

its own land, proved its disregard for treaties and in doing so kicked the ball back into the Russian court with enough force so that if it struck Putin's aid in his defensively outstretched hand Putin would still feel as if he had been kicked in the balls by a jackhammer. America had just stated that any further Russian aggression would only produce nuclear attacks which they could not equal. Due to the stated Treaty, the only nuclear weapons remaining to Russia were in the process of disassembly.

The radar began to come back online and Klinsky powered the reactor back into full activity watching as the pings on the radar became much more visible. It seemed as if pieces of static still remained, but when Klinsky looked upon a screen depicting the outside of the vehicle his heart nearly stopped. Within the near distance slowly rising was the exhaust trail of a missile and in the distance more trails were being formed as well.

"What just happened?" asked forward command.

"It looks like the US has launched a nuclear strike with missiles which our inspectors told us were in the process of decommissioning."

"So, Russia is fucked over."

"Yes. We are."

"Why did we do this anyway?"

"Hell, if I know."

That was presumably the moment that the Kremlin became not ash, but liquids and gasses as it felt an air burst and the radio signal fell silent. The exceedingly rapid destruction suggested that a submarine had launched the missile from the Baltic or North Arctic Sea.

A series of nearby explosions of nuclear class

deadened the tank's electronics making Klinsky jump to his feet in fear. He no longer could use his electronics to monitor the condition of the reactor, so he stood up and pulled a series of levers which released a series of counterweights rapidly retracting the rods from the reactor. Because he could not tell if they had retracted without his electronics, he began to test each crank to confirm the rods were fully retracted. The light within the room slowly faded as the fluorescents flickered amidst the rising static and popping from the radios.

The sensory array was essentially useless, no matter the work he could put into it. However, the reactor and the most important systems would be running within about two shifts of sixteen hours of work over two days.

***

Klinsky was awakened from a stupor-like slumber by the hideous grinding of some piece of equipment from above. He recalled the condition of his cameras and thus dashed out of the bunk room and looked up the ladder to the upper hatch of the vehicle, the only hatch which opened to the exterior. The sound arose from the hatch and yet no sparks were flying as Klinsky had expected. He reconsidered and determined that most likely they had not had time to get through the thick metal plating. The pins retracted at the biding of the steering wheel like handle as it began to slowly rotate counterclockwise with a low creaking sound. A drill, not a saw, had been applied.

"We are being boarded." Shouted Klinsky as the

hatch began to open disclosing a mass of fog that roiled in. The light of the sun was blocked by some unknown figure of an unarmored man wearing a respirator and a peculiar set of goggles. A coat flapped around him as he held an opened canister emitting a hiss of escaping gasses, which swirled amidst the tank, as the vaporous clouds above crept rapidly through the opening. The figure released the canister prompting Klinsky to jump back. The canister hit with its valve first causing the impact to shatter it, sending shrapnel scattering about striking sparks from whatever it hit. An entire side of the canister blew over Klinsky's head as cracked chips of metal clattered against the walls and pressurized, freezing, liquefied, noxious fumes spontaneously expanded outwards from the canister filling the craft with a potent noise of expanding gasses.

Within the gloom he saw abhorrent things of purple and black the most substantive of which was a winged silhouette without other discernible features apart from its general angularity, and then he blacked out as a purple flash filled his eyes.

***

He awakened upon some peculiar bed of stone his head resting upon a plush pillow and when he inhaled, he felt something hideous within his throat, like fire but slime. He opened his eyes as he jerked up to see that he was within the crater of a volcano and when he looked down, he saw lava rising slowly in a massive pool. He glanced around and saw an impossible series of vertical anvil plateaus which rose above the lava as it rolled and boiled upwards, engulfing more and more of the anvil plateaus in an inexorable hungry crawl.

Klinsky stood up looking down, weighing his fear of heights against his fear of burning to death, and decided that the devil loves a self-doubter. He began to run and made the leap of faith half a story to the next platform and felt himself beginning to fall to one side, but he continued, knowing that the way he had landed he should have annihilated some portion of his skeleton. He made the second jump and the third slowly climbing and jumping across three- and four-foot sections but on the fifth he found himself falling too fast and was struck in the lower abdomen by the ledge with enough violence to cause his bladder to let go. He felt hot warmth running down his legs and heard it hissing far away upon the boiling rock below. Klinsky had never been a strong man, but he managed to clamber back onto the plateau and found that he was a single jump away from a ledge on the side of the volcano's crater, yet it would be impossible for him to reach it. It was nearly at head height and five feet away from where he stood. He knew that he had a chance of catching it in his hands, but was that a risk he could take? Yes. He took the leap and felt his fingers slip below the ledge as his toes caught upon the wall and caused him to suddenly flip backward falling toward a fear he knew then was all too present. When he hit the lava, it tore beneath him as if it were merely hot tin foil, forced upward by a rising current of air as the light of some immense red globe shone down upon it, giving the foil such an appearance as it had.

He hit a soft, cold and wet surface putting out the burning of his back. He was lying upon snow and the bubble of lava had spontaneously transformed into swaying snowflakes. He got up and looked around, seeing a snow girt farm which he recognized as his own left behind when Russia went to war or did that ever happen, seeing as there was a flag of Finland on the flagpole placed upon the post supporting the roof over the front porch. He began to run towards his front door and stumbled upon the bottom step slamming his knee into the top causing him to let out a cry of pain.

Suddenly he realized, without knowing why, how much of a mistake he was making in making any noise at all. As he got up, he could not stop thinking of a particularly American pop culture reference of, "Ghouls." He turned as he arose and remembered the relevance. They were the original zombies and he turned back to the door knowing the irrationality of the notion until he noticed that there was no smoke coming from the chimney. He turned seeing vines growing over an old tractor and then noticed a single spot of color in the cold winter night in the form of a neon purple American muscle car with chrome trim and a black stripe down the side. Even this traditionally eardrum blasting vehicle rolled silently on down the back road to which the gravel driveway connected.

Purple. There was some peculiar relevance of purple, yet Klinsky did not have time to consider it. He slowly trod the stairs paying close attention to his footing when he heard the door creak. Out of the corner of his eye as he looked up he saw that the flag had become the Union Jack whilst he had been looking away, and that it transformed, with a rippling of somehow irksome structure, it became an American flag. His son came running out towards him crying, with a wrist missing, the stump covered in burns and blisters.

He was crying silently when Klinsky saw into his mouth, as the child opened it releasing a slight keening noise. He saw that his tongue had been cut out as well as an incision made upon his throat. Klinsky shrieked and stood up as the door banged open again disclosing the tooth mark ravaged corpse of his wife holding a kitchen knife up in the ice pick grip preparing to bring it down upon Klinsky who screamed again. He fell back blacking out before awakening within a plastic chair which shrilled upon a tile floor as he jerked violently.

Two men were before him, one sitting and one tall, pale man with a set of goggles hanging from his neck. They were the same goggles as the man who had dropped the canister into the Russian tank. This particular one spoke to the other with a British voice, somehow cultured and contemptuous of others – but retaining an American cadence and a somewhat jarringly coarse aspect which seemingly would be contradictory to the aforementioned British nature, "Do you want to know about how the tank worked?"

"No."

Klinsky broke in with his broken English pronunciation, "What the hell did you do to me!?" before continuing to shout incoherently due to overwhelming emotion.

The tall man looked at his associate, "Should I shut him up?"

"Yes, you have your fun with him. Seeing as he is a mere technician, we have no need for him."

Klinsky had no time to consider the tall man's words before he found himself sitting within a spacious old-fashioned vehicle, probably 1970 muscle, just like that muted machine in his last tormentation except this one was orange and black. The locks on the doors were all up and formed of chrome which contrasted perfectly with the wood and brown leather of the interior. Despite the beauty Klinsky did not want to be within the machine. He jerked his hand toward the door latch and before he could touch it the lock snapped down. He redirected his gaze to the passenger door lock and saw it snap downward audibly adding a totality to the feeling that he would never escape into the star filled night within the wooded locale. A black hotrod with red fire painted on the few remaining portions of its hood, which disclosed the oversized engine, pulled up beside Klinsky who had determined he was in a 1970 Challenger. The Challenger's gauges all pulsed red, and their needles cycled over to the right and back before the engine roared.

Klinsky attempted to roll down the window, but it was jammed, and the radio lit up as the interior lights went out leaving temporary red arcs where their filaments were still hot enough to emit light. The radio beat to a series of golden oldy AC-DCs before cycling to something in which modern heavy metal paled in comparison. When Klinsky looked back out upon the night he saw that they were on a four-lane highway's right side with a red light still glowing red above them. The stick of the Challenger slipped left and forwards. The green light turned on and both the vehicles roared as the clutch of the Challenger released itself, and each vehicle slammed forward. The Challenger's headlights snapped on with the sound of lightning as they bathed the world in a brilliant radioactive purple.

Each vehicle geared up simultaneously and yet neither had gained upon the other, but the Challenger's Christine style self-operation, each control operating itself without the bidding of any external forces, trumped the manual operation of the other driver and the Challenger gained by a foot as the vehicles continued ahead. A hill was climbed and then descended, and the road narrowed to two lanes and yet the hotrod pulled into the oncoming lane as if there was no danger of collisions.

The cars, still with their initial places, passed a small gun shop as they howled down a slope which terminated at a bridge. The bridge was an ugly construction of concrete crossing a portion of a lake and from it was visible great swaths of pristine, untainted land and yet the vehicles were beyond the bridge within a second slamming up another hill. There was a flash of purple, and the Challenger disappeared, leaving Klinsky with his momentum propelling him forward. The road curved left beneath him before gravity pulled him down. The opposing hotrod hit its brakes as the purple headlights of a square framed semi rose out of a sudden fog wall.

The semitruck and the hotrod sandwiched Klinsky, and yet there was no pain. All he felt was his heart beating more and more slowly as a peculiar sensation of hot liquid flowed within his chest. He soon expired, yet he knew that he was not dead. He felt himself in a thousand other realities in out-of-control situations knowing that he was within some monstrous stomach of an unknowable beast. A beast feeding upon every feeling, every memory, every fear and every single infinitesimal thing that was Klinsky's mind, stripping every charge from his secrets to fuel whatever predator had engulfed him. He knew that he was being digested and he knew that all the other 'hims' knew for they were him in different scenarios. His mind had been forced to multitask to an astonishing extent and it was dying as energy was stripped from it. The circuitry of the mind turned out to be constructs of energy, which too were ripped apart and off, slowly dissecting Klinsky's accumulated systems of thought process, leaving only a worthless husk of hardware.

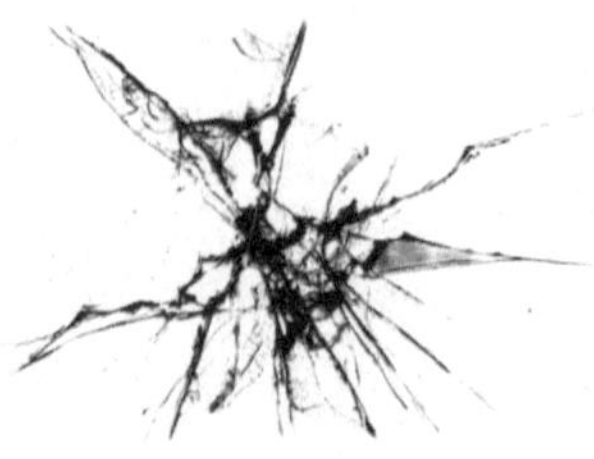

Terror at Night
by Phoebe Humpton

Claws grip my chest making it hard to breathe. I'm shaking and everything around me is blurry. Panic is all I feel. It surges through my body, and I squeeze my eyes shut to block everything out. It doesn't work. The pressure in my head is unbearable, like the world is pressing in on me, too close. Demons are attacking me. Scratching my arms and legs and engulfing me with their darkness. I feel myself getting smaller and smaller, trying to escape the demon's grasp. It is not working. Why isn't it working? Suddenly, through the panic and fear, I feel something else.

It's white hot, blazing in the darkness.

Anger.

I feel it in the pit of my stomach, but then it starts to spread through my whole body and zipping through my veins. The anger fills me up, and it's like someone splashed cold water over me; the water clearing out the fog that had gathered in my mind. Angry that I'm letting myself get smaller and smaller, that I'm not standing up, grabbing the demon by the neck, and chucking it into a wall. New strength surges into my limbs and I uncurl from my ball. I look around and see that I'm in circle of light that was being illuminated by a light hanging over my head. Past the circle of light was inky darkness. I couldn't see any walls in the black, but it felt like I was in a room so there had to be walls somewhere. For the first time I got a good look at the demons. Their heads were oval with short snouts. Horns parachuted from the top of their skull. The bodies of the demons looked like a cat, except the tail which ended in a point like a normal devil tail. The eyes which were just white holes, bore into me. The whole creature was black other than the eyes. In all my panic I hadn't realized how small they were, only about the size of a common house cat. Seeing this, I do what I should have done a long time ago.

I wrap my hands around the closest one's neck and hurl it as hard as I can into the darkness. Somewhere there was the sound of it hitting a wall. I turn toward the other demons and grab two, more flinging them away from me. I do this over and over again, getting into a rhythm. Grab, throw, grab, throw. I did it until there were no more demons. A smile spreads across my face. I did it. I'm safe now because I did something to protect myself. All of a sudden, I'm falling.

My eyes snap open, and I sit straight up in bed. My bed. In my room.

Everything was a dream.

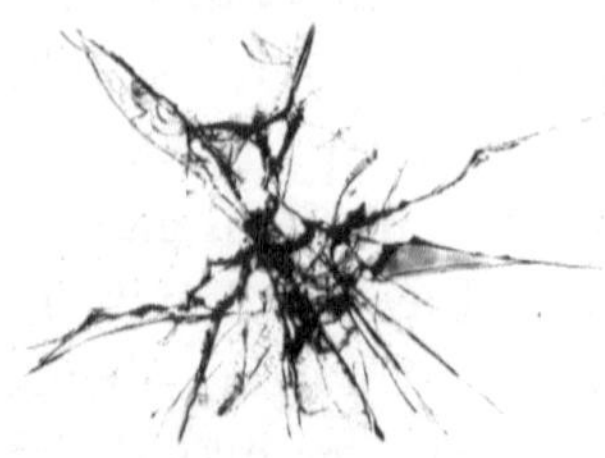

The American Grocery
by Kenning Spath

I was walking through the produce section of the local grocery, hands tip-tapping against my thighs. I felt nervous, which wasn't unusual for me, but more today than ever. I was having a relative in from out of town and was beginning to feel the usual stress one tends to have when preparing for guests. I hadn't seen my uncle Joey in months, and it would be good to see him again. I wanted to surprise him with his favorite treat. For some reason he always loved to have a good apple and some peanut butter.

He was the kind of man who was easy to please. Whose mouth, end to end, longed to stretch itself upward in joy. I, myself, wasn't a fan of this treat, but I indulged him whenever I could. When we got together it was only ever for a brief time, though they were always among my best memories. He worked a busy schedule and didn't get a lot of time off. I treasured my time with him. My uncle had practically raised me since my parents were never there. But after I moved away to go off to college, we hadn't had much contact. Before I left, he had given me his old leather jacket. He told me he used to be a "bad boy" when he was younger and that this completed the look. I always laughed when he told me this, but I wore the jacket every day. It felt good to always have my uncle with me. Like I was certain of something.

This is what I thought about as my hands picked through the apples. A lot of them were bruised, but I suppose that was just because it wasn't the right time of year for apple growing. As I looked through them, a beautiful, round red apple caught my eye. I smiled, picturing my uncle's face when he saw it. His round face would turn red and smile a big wide comforting smile. The kind of smile that would wrap its arms around me. I reached for one of the tear-away produce bags and struggled to find the opening for a minute. After some effort, I placed the apple in the bag and treated it as if it was my most valued possession. Now for the peanut butter.

I walked through the store until I reached the peanut butter. As my feet swept across the floor, they made a squeaking sound. I had mistakenly walked across some spilled soda. My eyes aimed at the ceiling, expressing their frustration in their own special way. Shaking my head, I proceeded to the aisle desired. Immediately I reached for the Jif, a smile once again big on my face. My uncle loved Jif.

Making my way to the register, cart now full of the necessary supplies, I reached my cashier, Jonas. He had been working there to help pay his way through college. He looked bored as usual, but we struck up our typical banter. I was in the middle of telling him about my dinner plans with my uncle, when we were both engulfed by the wave of confusion. All around me shoppers started to scream and fall to the ground. I stood there, vision blurring, as people fell to the floor around me. I heard shattering glass and the sound of firecrackers. My mind faintly registered that it was the middle of March and firecrackers hardly made any sense.

Instinctively, I dropped to the ground, clutching the apple protectively to my chest. Around me, wide-eyed shoppers shimmied across the ground. I was dazed and confused, and it felt like the world was falling apart around me. That's when I heard the firecrackers again. Only this time I realized they weren't firecrackers. As the gunshots rang out around the quiet local grocery, people desperately tried to flee and hide.

I saw the gunman, an impassive man, going about his business. His face expressionless as he fired round after round upon the crowd of people trying to get away. I realized I was crying. My face wet with tears, falling onto the floor. On the ground next to me there were already unmoving bodies. As I crawled, attempting to get to the bathrooms and hide, I saw the people lying motionless around me.

An elderly man (was he a grandfather?) lay motionless on the ground a few feet away. The cashier, with whom I had just been conversing lay sprawled out on the floor, limbs splayed out at odd angles, as if they had become separate from the rest of him. Old Man Cootie, the store manager, the man who had just been restocking the shelves by the checkout lines and who I'd known for years, lay unmoving too.

As I made my way desperately to the bathroom, an image burned into my brain. The flag pin that Cootie had insisted on wearing every day was catching the buzzing fluorescent lights. He was a veteran, displaying his love for his country and love for his home. I don't think he ever thought he would survive combat, risking his life for his country, only to die in a grocery store.

Was this what he had fought for?

I wasn't going to make it to the bathroom stalls. I knew that. I heard the firing at my feet as the man went about his terrible work, as if it was no trouble to him at all. I leapt to my feet, making a final bid for the bathrooms, when I felt the white-hot stabbing pains in my back. Desperately, I clutched the apple to my chest. Thinking of my uncle, and the dinner we were going to have tonight. I couldn't let it fall and bruise; he always liked a perfect apple. There were tears in my eyes as I crumpled to the ground, the apple, despite my best efforts, falling from my hand. I saw the bruises on it already, the once smooth red surface injured. Its inside juices bleeding out on the ground as surely as I would.

Already it was getting harder to think, my mind blissfully blocking the worst of the pain. I think it's funny how our minds numb us at the end. I suppose it's a kindness. I heard sirens outside in the distance. The police were here to save us. But they were too late. They were always too late.

As I breathed my last breaths, I thought of my uncle arriving at the airport and getting off the plane. He would of course be tired and cramping. He hated flying. But he always did it for me. I thought of him getting to the baggage claims area and looking around expectantly for me after locating his single bag. He would have his arms spread wide greeting me expectantly, ready to wrap me in a bear hug that would crush my lungs. Already I could see the disappointment and confusion as he found no one there. I could see the worry. I could see the growing concern as he turned his gaze to the airport TV and watched the breaking news.

"Wait!" I called out to my uncle. "I'm here! It's me!"

He turned to me and smiled that big smile of his and wrapped me in his arms. I hugged my uncle one last time as my eyelids grew heavy, lying on the floor of the local grocery.

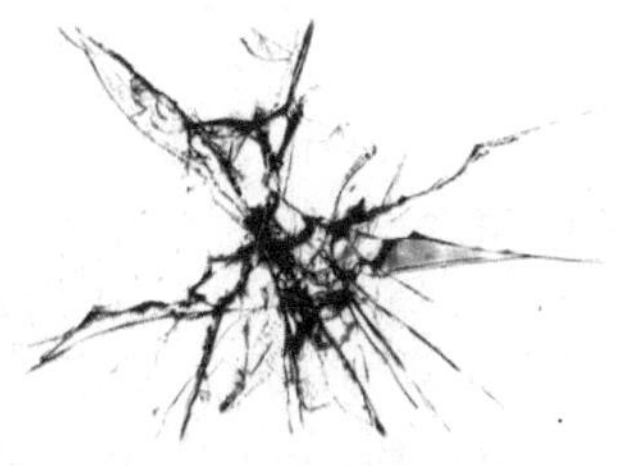

The Fear of Losing You
by Priscilla David

Reya always wondered which of her birthdays she loved most. There was her sweet sixteen, when Granny Mary and Grace Maxwell traveled from New York City to surprise her at her party. Well, her eighteenth birthday was a blast, notwithstanding the fact that her hero didn't make it.

Raymond Maxwell, a businessman based in New York City, the only son of Mary Maxwell, was Reya's dad—her hero. Raymond had been on a business trip to Nigeria when he got involved in an accident at work, and he had to be rushed down to a hospital in Abuja, Nigeria. A doctor was assigned to examine him, and later he was tended to by a nurse called Rihanna, whose ravishing beauty had captivated him. They exchanged contacts, and that was how the love story began. In a few years, they got married and birthed a lovely soul; Reya was her name.

Reya was the only child for eighteen years, and Raymond had always made it a priority to see his family in Nigeria, not less than twice in a year. Rihanna, being a nurse, meant many shifts at work, and for this reason, Reya was alone most of the time. She'd often stay indoors all day long. She had her library at home, which was the favorite part of the house for her. Angel Daniels was Reya's bestie, but their worlds weren't all the same. Angel loved hanging out a lot and had little or no time to spend all day with her books. At school, Reya was quite popular amongst the nerds; she was so brilliant.

The door to Reya's study creaked, and there was Rihanna, smiling so sweetly.

"Hi darling. Can you please help me do the laundry? I'll join you shortly."

Reya was sorting the colors from the others.

"How did school go today?" Rihanna questioned, picking a sachet of powdered detergent from a shelf. She emptied most the contents into the washing machine.

Reya dumped the colored clothes in the machine and turned the knob.

"Same old story, I had a normal day at school being the most popular nerdy kid in class and having to face the embarrassment of stuff like not knowing who sang some trending songs and all that. Thanks to Angel and her cool group of friends who wouldn't just stop blabbing about absolute nonsense. How's that any of my business, by the way?"

Rihanna held Reya's cheeks delicately in her both hands.

"Being a nerd isn't something bad. Those kids don't just know how powerful you are up there. Typically, they're nerds, they're obsessed over the teenage world and that's what they don't understand." She tapped Reya's head. "You are special, I want you to always remember that darling."

Reya sighed, saying to herself, If only everyone would understand that.

"There's something special to share with you. Let's go get a glass of juice, don't you think so?"

Reya shrugged and followed her mom through to the dining room where her mom poured them both two glasses of apple juice.

"What's it about, Mom?" Reya asked.

Rihanna smiled. "Why don't you take a guess, darling?"

"Nooooo!" Reya whined. "I'm not good at guesses, Mommy."

A laugh escaped Rihanna's lips. "Fine. We'll be going to America soon! Your dad has invited us over."

A big wave of energy coursed through Reya. "Oh my! Mommy, this is the best news that I've heard in months." she replied, hugging Rihanna tightly.

America was her dreamland. She had wanted to visit the beautiful places in America like Rochester, and reality was just a step away. But that was just the tip of the iceberg; this meant that Reya would be closer to her hero and her granny, Mary Maxwell, whom she greatly adored.

The news had made her day. Well, it seemed like some sort of fairy had glued a big smile on Reya's face for the whole day. Reya Maxwell's eighteenth birthday party was a lovely one. When she was getting prepped for the party, her mom walked in with a big, beautifully wrapped present. There was a card that read,

Happy birthday, sweetheart. You've been my greatest source of joy, and watching you grow has been a wonderful experience. Thank you for coming into my life. You own a big part of my heart, bigger than the landmark of Africa. I love you so much, baby, but I'm so sorry that I can't make it today; an appointment came up, and I couldn't miss it. But baby, this doesn't mean that work is more important to me than you are. You mean the whole world to me. Rock your day, sweetheart.

--Your dad, Raymond.

Reya burst into tears, hugging the card close to her chest. Then, she uncovered the box. Inside was the most gorgeous dress she had ever seen: an off-the-shoulder blush and gold ball gown, lying next a five-inch platform heels and a gold filigree purse.

"I love you, Dad," Reya cried out. "I love you so much.

Rihanna walked closer to her and pulled her into a tight hug. "Shhh. That's alright darling; Dad loves you too."

"I know, Mom. I wish I could give much more than he has given me. He is just so amazing. He's the best father that I can ever ask for."

Rihanna patted her head.

"All you should do right now is to walk into that

bathroom, clean up, cheer up, and be the life of the party. You'll look beautiful in that dress." Rihanna winked.

It was literally a small party. Rihanna had invited a couple of friends and neighbors. Angel and her group of friends flooded the living room and the lounge. Music blasted through the house, and many of the guests were dancing.

With Rihanna and her friends being around, there was little to no glitch with the preparations and food. Snacks, drinks, and food were passed around at certain times. There so was much fun and presents for Reya.

Later, when Reya unwrapped her numerous presents, she just couldn't stop herself from gaping out loud. There were just so many beautiful things. Angel went as far as buying a collection of twelve books for her and another book titled Ladder to the Top which Reya had recently desired.

The next afternoon, Reya was alone at home. Rihanna had just left for work. So, when her phone rang, and her mom asked her to open the door, she was worried.

Outside stood the last people she was expecting, her hero and Aunt Grace.

"Daddy!" she screamed, jumping on him so swift that it caught him off-balance. He had to drop the luggage to hug Reya back. "Daddy, I missed you so much. I wasn't expecting you at all. What happened? Daddy, you don't know how happy I am right now. You should have seen me looking so beautiful, big and all grown yesterday..."

Grace frowned. "Excuse me. I never knew I was invisible."

Raymond and Reya laughed at the joke.

"Hello, Aunt." said Reya, hugging her. "I'm so sorry about that. I just wasn't expecting some august visitors."

Grace smiled warmly, making her way into the house. "Your dad wanted to make it a surprise."

Reya took a deep breath. "I've missed you all so much. Thank you for your present, Dad. I really do love it." She turned to Grace. "How was the flight?"

Raymond, Grace, and Reya chatted for a long time. When it was almost evening, Raymond and Reya ended up cuddling in bed together.

The next day, Reya and Grace had cooked up something delicious for breakfast. Raymond and Rihanna weren't going to join them because Raymond was taking his wife out on a date that morning. When Raymond and Reya came down the stairs, properly dressed for their outing, Reya and Grace were having breakfast. Everyone exchanged greetings. Rihanna had submitted her resignation letter from work yesterday, and all protocols had been duly observed.

After breakfast, Grace and Reya paid a visit to a big bookshop. For a birthday treat, Grace asked Reya to pick as many books as she wished and put the bill on her. And so, Reya kept adventuring the bookshop and laying hands on all genres of literature.

On the other hand, Raymond and Rihanna went around the city, visiting some tourist locations. Later, they had lunch with old friends around the city where Raymond discussed his big plans for his family, courtesy of a contract worth big bucks, and everyone was awed. Then, they had to get a few things for themselves and the girls.

On their way home that evening, there was a sweet feeling of joy bubbling in Raymond's heart, and he could practically visualize a beautiful future…waking up to his wife's beautiful face every day and having his daughter around him always. Thanks to the big contract which he had bagged recently.

When Raymond glanced briefly at his wife, he could see something in her eyes. "What's going on, Anna? You don't look alright, honey."

She said again. "I feel so uneasy right now. I don't just know why, but I will be alright."

"Are you sure about that?" Raymond questioned. He reached across and held Rihanna's hand, steering the wheel with just one hand. "Thanks for hanging out with me today, Anna." said Raymond, squeezing her hand, lightly.

Rihanna sighed. "I should be saying that Ray. Thank you for coming into my life and for giving me every reason to smile whenever I see you."

When Raymond looked ahead again, there was a trailer coming towards them at a surprisingly high speed. Raymond tried swerving and doing all he could but there was no way out. And the last words he kept hearing was, Lord, I do not want to leave my child alone in this cruel world, just yet. Help me.

He wished he could do something to help his beloved wife. But all he knew was pure pain and then, the world went blank.

When Desmond Samuel, Rihanna's brother, got a call from his sister's workplace, he was confused. He got into his beat-up Sienna and drove down to the hospital.

"Hello, I am Desmond Samuel, and I just received a call right now requesting to see me urgently," he said as soon as he got to the reception booth.

"Please, come with me. Doctor Ken would like to see you."

Desmond was uneasy. As soon as he was sitting across from Doctor Kennedy, whom he had known through Rihanna, he demanded to know what the problem was.

"Desmond, I don't know where to start from." He sighed, clasping his hands. "She was involved in a fatal accident and was rushed down here. For now, all I know is that she was in the passenger seat, and the driver is unidentified as he was burnt and charred."

Desmond frowned. "Who are you talking about, Ken?"

"I know this is hard to believe, but we lost her... we lost Rihanna."

Desmond looked up and tears ran down his face. He stood up and went out of the room going to nowhere exactly. After a while he came back inside and requested to see Rihanna's corpse. He was told that he had to pay a huge sum of money for all the life-support materials and medications that Rihanna had used before her death. On hearing the outrageous sum, Desmond was downcast, because as at that time his twin kids were about to seek admission into the university, and besides, he had four other kids to care for.

After leaving the hospital, he went straight to the Maxwell home, where Grace opened the door. "Hi Desmond, what are you doing here? I've been so worried. I've tried calling Ray and Rihanna, but I just can get through to them. They ought to have been home by now.

Desmond sighed and walked over to a couch."Where is Reya?"

"She in her study room," Grace replied sitting across from him.

Then, he broke the news, and Grace had to muffle down a scream.

"Wait a second, what did you just say, Uncle?

They looked up at the stairs, and there was Reya, a shattered look on her face. Grace and Desmond tried all they could to comfort Reya, but she didn't stop crying that evening, and when she woke up the next day, her eyes were all red and swollen.

In a couple of days, Grace and Reya were on their flight to America, and Granny Mary welcomed them warmly upon their arrival.

"My darling, you look so beautiful, just like your mother. Welcome home"

Reya was shown to her room, and when she later came downstairs to eat, Grace and Granny Mary were having a little chat on the dining table.

"Ray and Rihanna just had to stay a little longer for a vacation together, and I believe...."

Reya cleared her throat all attention were on her.

Granny Mary beckoned. "Come over here darling. I cooked something I know you would like; I can't wait for Anna and Ray to come over. They have to tell me about the secret behind birthing such a beautiful young lady like you, darling."

There was a tight lump in Reya's throat. She quietly took a seat from across Grace and allowed Granny to dish her food

She went to bed early and cried herself to sleep. The following morning, while Grace went to the supermarket, Granny walked into Reya's room, where Reya was staring up into nothingness.

"What is going on, darling? You don't seem okay. Please, talk to Granny."

Reya sighed. "I'm just tired and not used to this environment. I'm just adapting" Granny smiled "I have an idea. I cooked sauced and peppered meat for you. Let's go downstairs, and while we eat, you can tell me about your party."

Reya reluctantly got up from her bed and went along with Granny Mary's plans.

"So, how was the party? I had missed every bit of the party. Tell me about the presents you received. What did your mom and dad gift you? Did you love that gorgeous dress that Ray had bought? You should have seen him getting all worked up about your party." Granny laughed.

Reya's chest felt so heavy, and her eyes watered. She bit her cheeks hard to hold down the tears, but they unconsciously streamed down her cheeks. That confirmed Granny's suspicions: nothing was all alright.

Something was wrong somewhere, no doubt. "Reya, can you please talk to me? Tell me what this is all about."

Reya spilled it all out and out of the blue, Granny fainted. Reya immediately reached across to Grace, who was already in neighborhood. She was so scared to lose her. Granny Mary was rushed down to the hospital where she was attended to.

Now, things would never be the same again. Granny Mary mourned their deaths and tried to stay strong for her only grandchild. On the other hand, Grace had moved back to London to go on with her life and work. Schools were about to start, and Reya ought to begin college.

With no funds available, Granny Mary had to engage in menial jobs that she had never dreamt of doing at her age. She worked at the homes of the wealthier citizens as a babysitter, as a home aid, and at some other times, she simply did all she could do. But all of these weren't bringing forth the desired sum of money. For this reason, Granny Mary made some contacts and took the only option which was available because all she wanted was for her grandchild to be happy, and she was ready to do all it took to send Reya to Cornell University, not minding the fact that her only friend, Shelly, wasn't willing to help her out, even though she could literally help…this saddened Granny Mary.

All Reya knew was that her grandmother travelled to Asia to visit old friends, and she soon returned with a huge sum of money that could afford her tuition fees into Cornell University, and there was so much more that could be invested in other things.

Life in college was not what Reya had anticipated. She had always dreamt of herself being the perfect role model figure at school…the professor's good girl whom everyone would love to be friends with. Her parents' death had seriously affected her; she wasn't interested in social activities at school, and all she ever wanted to do was to absorb herself in every book she could lay her hands on. All she wanted to do was to stay at the top of the department, to prove her mother right, that she was special, and to make her granny proud.

She would often catch some people rolling their eyes when she walked into class, just because she was smart, and she wasn't friends with anyone at school. She practically avoided everyone and hated going to social gatherings. When the semester ended, Reya was glad to go back home, to the only family she now had.

Reya opened the door to their house and surprisingly, there was no one at home. She began to panic and immediately called Granny Mary, but she couldn't get across to her and so, she contacted Grace.

"I'd be right there with you, Reya. Hold on, don't go anywhere." Grace came around and picked Reya up.

"Where are we going, and where is Granny?"

"You'll find out," said Grace.

When Grace parked in front of a hospital, not far from the house, Reya's heart was aching.

"We'd like to see Mary Maxwell," said Grace to the receptionist.

He replied, "Room 29."

Grace and Reya were offered seats at a distance from Granny Mary, who looked so pale and weak.

"Reya? My darling, I've missed you so much," said Granny Mary, her voice cracking up.

Reya was so confused. "Granny, what happened?" she questioned, breaking down into tears. Seeing her grandmother like this was so painful for her. "You don't deserve to be here."

Granny Maxwell shook her head, tears gathering in her eyes. "Reya, I'm so sorry to put you through this. I only wanted you to be happy, darling."

"What do you mean?" Reya's head ached so much.

"I promised myself after your father's death to always see you smile, and I knew that Cornell was where you wanted to be. All I could do was to sell one of my kidneys, and now, I don't have what exactly it takes to fight Covid. I'm so sorry, darling."

Reya kept bawling. "Granny, you shouldn't have done that. This is all my fault; I wish you hadn't done that. I could just have waited for a year so that we could raise money without putting your life at risk. I'm nothing but ill luck to everyone. Because of me, my parents died, and now…I just hate myself."

Reya ran out of the room. She had made up on mind on what to do. She felt a pair of arms pull her back, right at the moment when she thrust herself towards the road. Those pair of arms belonged to Grace, who was holding her firmly and pulling her back to the driveway. Reya kept crying into her aunt's shoulder.

"You shouldn't have stopped me, Aunt, I want to die. I do not deserve you guys."

Grace shook her head.
"Don't say that love; the world needs you. We all need you.

I looked around and discovered that

People do not believe in themselves anymore

They see themselves as a burden to the world

They now think the world does not need them

Why not then heal the world

And cause less pain to your beloveds

In tears, I call people who think

They're the worst of their kinds

To come together and see what the world loses

When they're gone

It's all about the mind

You have to direct your mind before you lose focus

The world needs you

Heal the world with your God-given potentials

Don't decrease the world,

Rather heal the world in greatness

And with your potentials

Look back and see people who love and care about you

And find out that the world needs you

You are the world

You and the world are like rain and water

Do your best to heal the world as one

And always remember

If you fall a hundred times,

You'll rise up stronger."

3 YEARS LATER

"The best students this year are Eric Hall, Reya Maxwell, Natasha Wolff…"

When Reya walked up to receive her award, she could see her Granny Mary and Aunt Grace cheering her on. Yes, Granny Mary had fought and survived. When they exited the hall with big smiles on their faces, they all had every reason to celebrate for their latter victory.

"Hello, excuse me, Miss Maxwell."

Reya turned to see a beautiful woman smiling sweetly at her, and right beside her was a smart-looking, aging man. She gracefully walked towards Reya and hugged her.

"Congratulations, my nerd. You made it."

It was a big hit on Reya. She stumbled backwards, her eyes tearing up. "Mom?" she croaked.

Grace and Granny Mary both gaped. "Rihanna?"

Rihanna nodded, holding back tears. "It's me." She looked at her crying daughter, who was now a full-grown woman, and she burst into uncontrollable tears. "We need to talk."

They all made their way to Granny Mary's house. As soon as they were settled, Rihana began.

"This man by my side is Mr. Blake. He's the president of the hospital where I worked. On that unfortunate day, Mr. Blake had a few things to take care of at the headquarters at Abuja, where I worked. So, when I was rushed in and word went round that I, one of their most excellent nurses, needed urgent care, a team of doctors was assigned to take care of me.

When Mr. Blake, through my file, he found out that I was daughter to Mr. and Mrs. Samuel, kind souls who had been there for him and his family when everything was not in their favor, when the world was almost crumbling against him and his family. Today, he is a great man to reckon with in the medical field around the society. He felt indebted and wanted to pay back the favor. So, he put me on life support and did everything to keep me alive. The plan was to claim a fake death and proclaim a very huge amount of money, which successfully, my brother couldn't afford. So, when I finally woke up last year, I underwent some plastic surgeries, and here I am today, hale and hearty. Thanks to Mr. Blake."

Reya couldn't help tears pouring from her eyes.

Rihanna said. "Baby, I am so proud of what you have become, and I am deeply sorry for all the pain that you went through." Rihanna pulled Reya to herself and hugged her tightly.

"We'll be fine; we now have each other. That's all that matters. I love you, baby."

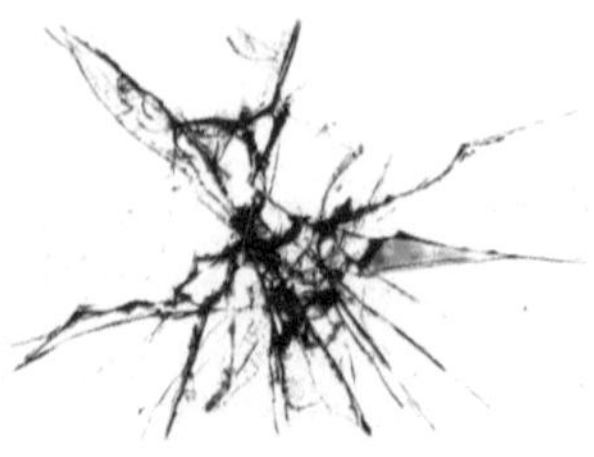

Route
by Ainslee Davenport

Hot dog or sandwich?

Hesitation froze Alfie to the GoStop floor. He glanced over at the cashier. She was on her phone, but he couldn't help but think she was staring at him moments prior. Or someone else was. His eyes flittered around the gas station. It was empty. Still, he couldn't shake the feeling of eyes on him.

The paranoia forced his hand forward to snatch up the hot dog.

There was a certain fear in knowing that some things are out of your control. There was also a certain comfort.

Alfie knew that he was either going to die or go back. This was out of his control.

The fear made him shake. The comfort kept him from passing out.

He hurried over to the counter feeling for the coins in the back pocket of his jeans. His fingers brushed against the flash drive and he shuddered.

Alfie's gaze caught on the candy shelf. He…really wanted a chocolate bar. He counted the coins in his hand. He had enough money. But should he?

"You good, dude?"

Alfie jolted. He barely caught himself on the edge of the shelf instead of crashing into the display. The cashier didn't look concerned, thankfully.

"Yeah." Alfie's voice cracked. "Yeah."

Quickly grabbing a chocolate bar, he shuffled over on shaky legs and dumped the items onto the counter.

He handed the cashier his pile of coins, his bounty of a gas station hot dog and chocolate bar sitting on the counter, waiting to be scanned.

One last meal, he thought wryly. He had to tamp down the hysterical laughter that tried to bubble up his throat.

Alfie fumbled with the bag and change he was handed.

The cashier probably thought he was on drugs. Alfie certainly looked the part with ratty clothes and bloodshot eyes, showing up at three o'clock in the morning and paying in dirty coins.

The assumption was technically right. Paranoia was one powerful drug.

They probably got a lot of drug addicts at this run-down GoStop in the middle of nowhere, though, judging by the cashier's general unaffected and disinterested attitude, even as Alfie stumbled into a stand filled with chips on his way to the door.

He would be surprised if that was true. This area wasn't exactly idyllic.

If he was unlucky, death might snatch him up even quicker than expected, stabbed to death in a sketchy GoStop parking lot for his literal pocket change. Or lucky, depending on how you looked at it.

Luckily—or unluckily, again depending on how you looked at it—the small parking lot was deserted. Still, that did nothing to soothe Alfie's paranoid thoughts as he sat down on the curb. The cold of the concrete soaked through the seat of his jeans. He couldn't stop the way his eyes darted around and his ears perked up at every minute sound. His hair stood on end, even as he viciously tore into the hot dog's packaging.

The hot dog disappeared quickly. It was soon followed by the chocolate bar. The sweetness melted on his tongue and he missed it as soon as it was gone. He wished he had savored it a little more. Now with his stomach full and his heart a little emptier, the urge to lay back completely on the frigid concrete and let himself waste away was harder to ignore.

Alfie contemplated going back inside and getting another chocolate bar. He barely had enough money left over for it. However, it wouldn't be good if the cashier were to think that a crackhead coming back for a second time broke into the territory of suspicion. The cashier didn't seem bothered the first time, but Alfie of all people knew how people could change their minds at the drop of a hat.

Alfie sighed lowly, breath fogging in front of his face and stood up with a quiet groan.

He shook out his limbs and headed for the trees. Time to go. A shortcut through the trees will be quicker.

The woods were pitch black. With the thick foliage overhead, little light would penetrate even in the daytime. Now the moon was barely a sliver in the night sky, and Alfie could barely see his hands if he lifted them in front of his face.

Alfie was sure if anyone could see him in the darkness, he would look idiotic with his arms outstretched to feel for trees and his feet inching forward with every step to not trip on roots.

Immediately after crossing the tree line and into the oppressing darkness, he began to regret his decision. Alfie was never a fan of the dark, always preferring night lights to complete darkness as a child. Now with all of the threats looming over him, he disliked it even more.

His skin crawled with the thought of all of the bugs and spiders that must be hidden in the dark and the thought of who could be watching him, waiting to finally catch him unaware in a place he could not be vigilant.

The harsh comfort of impending, unavoidable death had faded sometime between leaving the GoStop and stumbling blindly over roots and rocks in the dark, leaving him only with cold, nauseating fear. Frantically making his way through the trees, Alfie finally admitted to himself a fact that he had been running from ever since he had started running: He did not want to die.
But it wasn't about what he wanted anymore. He doubted it ever was.

It seemed like hours—and it very well could have been—before the trees thinned and deposited Alfie onto the familiar path that he had been so desperately searching for.

His breath came out in short bursts. He was winded from traveling so far while being so out of shape. The relief that filled him cleared his mind enough for him to finally realize that he probably should have bought a flashlight at the GoStop.

Alfie didn't know whether he was more frustrated or amused with himself and his stupidity. Amusement at the irony won out, and he silently huffed out of his nose.

It truly was his own bad choices that led him here, stumbling in the dark.

Bending over with his elbows digging into his ribs, he pressed his palms into his eyelids with a soothing pressure and resisted the urge to sit down and give up. To let the wild animals, bugs, and other figures of his imagination finish him off. He shook himself harshly. That wasn't his choice to make.

Alfie set down the path with renewed fervor, fear tasting almost intoxicating on his tongue.

Time felt strange, refusing to compute in his brain, but some of it must have passed before the trees thinned again, then disappeared, revealing a small clearing. Alfie hurried to cross it. The space was too open for him to feel any resemblance of safety. He brokenly jogged over to the wooden walkway that was on the other side. The pathways had been built so hikers could get over the many small creeks that ran through the woods. A bit further down, the walkway breached out of the woods to sidle up against a river.

When he was smaller, Ms. Vang would take him here sometimes so he could get out of the stuffy townhouse they both called home. The area was secluded enough the fit Ms. Vang's tastes and open enough that Alfie could run freely across the wooden slats and try his luck at balancing on rocks to cross the water without getting drenched.

But now any water was almost frozen over and Alfie had neither the energy nor the desire to play around or explore.

Besides, he doubted there was much more adventure to be squeezed out of this particular place. After all the days he had spent exploring it during his childhood, he already knew it like the back of his hands. Perhaps better even, since he could barely recognize his hands through the scabs and grime that covered them.

His knowledge of the area was the whole reason he had come in the first place. To see if he could find some comfort in the familiarity in his last moments.

Alfie paused as dirt turned to wood beneath his feet. He closed his eyes and took a deep breath. He choked, grasping onto the rough railing hard enough to irritate his already scraped-up hand. His other hand lay limp at his side.

There was nostalgia in the air, and Alfie clung to it with wild desperation. He felt colder suddenly and not just from the freezing temperature. The nostalgia he breathed in burned his throat. It wasn't the comforting, soft feeling he had hoped for. It was a bitter nostalgia, soured by his fear.

This place had changed. So had Alfie. They no longer recognized each other.

Small tremors wracked Alfie's body. He leaned sideways against the railing. It was the only thing keeping him up now. His eyes were still closed tightly, and he floated in the darkness behind his eyelids. The ground pushing up against the soles of his feet and the way that the railing dug into his hand and side were the only things keeping him grounded.

Even the eerie sounds of the forest felt far away. Alfie felt far away. He recognized faintly that he could not bring himself to move his body, though his muscles still shook minutely—whether from the fear or the cold, he did not know.

A fear that he would not be able to make himself move in time trickled into him. What if—

Something was crawling on his hand.

A sharp terror tore through him and his eyes ripped open as he frantically shook his hand. Something flew off and fluttered around his face. Alfie stumbled back waving his hands around his face.

The thing flew slightly closer and his panic renewed until he realized… It was just a moth.

Alfie relaxed—not wholly, never wholly—as the adrenaline and fight left him.

It had just been a moth. Not the worst thing. Still, Alfie shuddered. He hated bugs.

Phantom insects crawled across his skin and Alfie was faintly grateful that it was winter as he scratched at his arms and neck. In the summer months, the woods were filled with so many bugs you could choke on them. He hadn't minded as much when he was a child, but now Alfie thought he would go insane if any more bugs besides the ones conjured up by his imagination were on him.

Alfie supposed he should be at least a tiny bit grateful for the moth, though, since he was no longer frozen to the railing. At least he could move now.

Alfie took another, slower deep breath, not daring to close his eyes this time. His gaze darted around from tree to tree, the darkness obscuring and warping them. He resisted the urge to glance over his shoulder, even as a paranoid shiver made its way slowly over his spine.

He wouldn't know what to do if he saw something anyway.

Alfie forced his feet to move, using the railing to guide himself. It was mostly a straight shot to his destination now with only a few twists and bends in the walkway. He moved forward, occasionally having to duck and lean to avoid running into overgrown branches that hung over the path.

An indiscernible amount of time passed. Alfie continued to walk. He doubted he would be able to move forward again if he stopped. If he paused even for a moment, fear would lock him in place.

The trees to his left thinned and then disappeared to reveal the river, wide and covered in chunks of ice.

Alfie turned on his heel to face it and paused to take in the sight. He clutched the railing tightly as something ugly turned in his stomach.

He had never come here in the winter before. His memories were filled with sun and heat. It didn't feel right to see it like this, still and silent like all life had been drained from it.

A sound came from behind and he whipped around to face it. There was nothing there. Alfie didn't know what to make of the slight disappointment that came along with the relief.

He shouldn't have come here. His fear and paranoia had taken root and spread, ruining what could have stayed a happy memory.

Alfie reached behind himself to feel for the railing. His fingers grazed the wood and he clutched it like a lifeline. He stumbled back and soon he was sliding down against the wooden boards. In a second, he was off his feet, leaning with his back and shoulders pressed against the wood.

A cough wracked his body and filled the air with fog.

His numb fingers fumbled with the flaps of his bag, and Alfie was barely able to fish out his phone without dropping it. He gazed blankly at the dark screen for a long moment before finally turning it on.

The brightness blinded him, and he closed his eyes instinctively against the burn. He forced them open again to peer at the screen.

He unlocked it.

He scrolled through the few contacts he had before finding the one he wanted.

Bronwyn Vang

The phone rang only twice before she picked up.

"Alfie," Ms. Vang said, her voice thick with sleep. "Why are you calling me?"

Her voice wasn't gentle. Nothing about Ms. Vang was gentle. Still, the sound of her voice soothed something deep inside of him in a way the forest could never.

"I just wanted to say goodbye." Alfie cleared his throat. His voice was rough from disuse when he spoke. "And to warn you. I didn't want you to be surprised."

"At this point, I'm more surprised you're still alive

to call me now." Clack. Clack. Clack. The faint sounds of beads moving against one another came through the phone. A wave of nostalgia flooded over him.

Alfie huffed out a silent laugh. She always was the sentimental sort. Unable or unwilling to let go of the past. That she still wore the beaded necklace he made her so long ago was just proof he didn't need.

He had started it here, actually. Quite a few beads were accidentally dropped through the wooden boards in the process. He had taken so long—between trying to meticulously place every bead on the string in the perfect order and trying to hide his project from Ms. Vang—that he had had to finish it on the car ride back. He still remembered the frustration and panic that had filled him every time Ms. Vang had glanced in the rearview mirror.

But he had finally finished the handmade jewelry and had presented it to her as soon as the car had stopped, jumping out of the car and saying, "I made you this." Are you proud of me, he meant.

Ms. Vang had inspected the colorful beads and then, looking very seriously into his eyes, said, "I'll treasure this forever." Yes, I am, she meant.

Somehow, knowing that she hadn't broken her promise stung worse than if she had.

"With you the way you are, I knew it would happen eventually."

A wry smile forced its way onto his cracked lips. She was the one who had made him this way.

But Ms. Vang was a stubborn creature. Refusing to see how things had changed. Refusing to see how Alfie had changed. Even after all these years, she still only saw "Alfie" as the little orphan boy she had taken in and regarded him as a stranger.

"Well." Alfie forced the words out through clenched teeth. "I'm glad you are prepared."

"Yes. I am too."

The Clack. Clack. Clack. grated at his nerves.

"Goodbye, Mom." Ms. Vang was not his mother. But she might as well have been.

A moment of silence on the other end.

Clack. Clack. Clack. "Goodbye."

Clack. Clack. —

The sound was interrupted by the disconnect tone. Silence laid heavy on his shoulders.

Bitterly, Alfie wondered if she had received the news with no warning—no previous preparation, just the news of his death—would she have had more of a reaction? Would she have mourned his death if she hadn't already mourned him while he was alive?
Because that was what she had always done, hadn't she? Any time he changed, she couldn't accept that, so she mourned the boy she knew and wrote off the one she could have met. She was so afraid of change that she couldn't accept him when he wouldn't stay the same.

Alfie was a Ship of Theseus. He had been torn down and replaced bit by bit until there was nothing left of the original. She only loved the ship she knew. It was a bit ironic, seeing as she was the one who rebuilt him. Ms. Vang couldn't realize how she was the one who had changed him.

Because Ms. Vang was not a gentle woman. She was stubborn and harsh, and Alfie had chosen to bend instead of break and be molded to her will. He had been rebuilt until all they both were left with was memories.

Ironic that she hadn't been happy with her own work.

But while Ms. Vang found comfort in control, Alfie found comfort in being controlled, and they had both comfortably walked that path until they ended up with a result neither one of them was happy with.

That was always the problem, wasn't it? Alfie was too afraid to be in control that he always chose to bend.

That was how he ended up here, with a thumb drive full of classified information burning a hole in his jeans pocket. Despite knowing exactly where he was, he was lost in the darkness without someone to tell him what to do. Just a puppet, limp and lifeless without someone to pull his strings.

Even with a clear ending in sight, he still didn't know what to do.

The information contained within the drive was dangerous. It could get people killed. Others, not just him.

He pulled the flash drive out with shaky fingers. So much power in such a small package. It was smaller than his thumb but was worth more than he was.

Despite his disobedience, he hadn't done anything irreversible yet. Alfie…still had time, still had a choice. They were still tracking him and would be here soon, but if he gave it back, if he completed his mission, he still had a chance. Or at least the illusion of one.

They might kill him anyway, just for his insubordination, but he doubted it. He was a powerful tool, made all the more valuable by how easily he was controlled.

Alfie may have broken free of their control this time, but they all knew if he went back, he wouldn't be able to repeat that stunt again. Things would go back to how they were. Comfortable.

But if he gave up the thumb drive, he wouldn't just be giving up information. He wouldn't just be giving up dozens—if not hundreds—of lives. He would be giving up himself again, only a gasping breath of freedom before he was dragged back under. And this time he would comfortably drown in the waves of their control.

Alfie was tired. He was tired of following orders. He was tired of letting others rip off his boards only to hammer down new ones. He was tired of siphoning himself off to others.

Choosing for himself was a frightening path, but running through the woods of his own volition was the first time he had felt alive in a while. He was still tired, but the same fear that made his hands shake and his heart pump faster with adrenaline made him feel wide awake.

The low hum of a vehicle reached his ears, making him flinch. They were here.

The one problem with his resting place was the dirt road nearby, leading to the river from the local highway. Only roughly a dozen trees separated him from the road.

The road had been barely used when he was a child, and he used to think that he and Ms. Vang were the only two in the world who knew about it.

The hum grew louder.

Alfie stood shakily, turning to face the frozen river. His legs tried to buckle, but he forced himself to stand.

He could do this one thing for himself. He could make this one choice.

Everyone has to work with the life they are allotted, and Alfie had allowed others to use his. The last few days were the first time in a while he had used his life for himself. It was time to take back a few more seconds.

The hum stopped. A car door slammed. Voices. With shaking hands, Alfie made his choice. The flash drive disappeared into the icy water below.

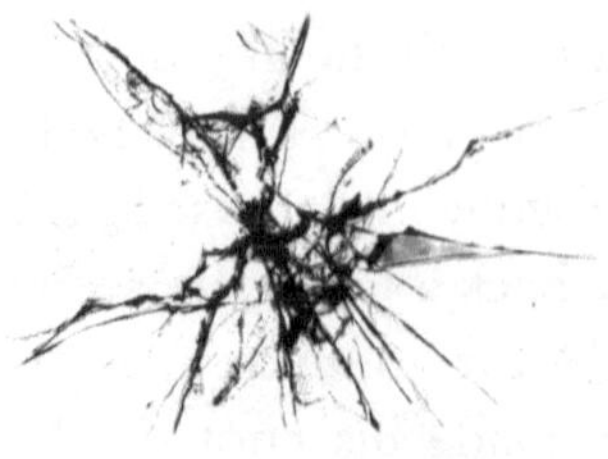

The Authors

Gracie Lockey

Gracie Lockey lives in Palm Coast, Florida with her six cats and three dogs. She is a playwright, novelist, and poet. Gracie is on the Autism Spectrum and has been diagnosed with ADHD and Anxiety. Gracie hopes to one day see her work get produced/on the New York Times Bestseller list, however, she will know she really succeeded when there is fan fiction based on her writing.

Logan Farmer

Logan is a ninth grade student with the interests of writing books and reading. He has no previous publishing experience however he is currently working on writing a fantasy YA novel. That also comes along with random things he writes in his free time. The demographic Logan aims for is from ages twelve and up.

Sky Corkern

Sky Corkern is a 14 year old who hails from New Orleans Louisiana and currently resides in Texas. She has been a writer from the moment she could hold a pen, she has written countless stories songs and hopes to soon combine her love of baking with writing and publish her first cookbook. In her spare time she also enjoys singing painting, painting, and spending time with her family.

Liam Lamont

Liam Lamont is a teen writer who lives in semi-rural Georgia with his parents and three insane siblings. In his spare time, he enjoys video editing, reading, and camping. He is currently working on a full novel which he hopes to publish in the near future.

Elizabeth O. Ogunmodede

Elizabeth O. Ogunmodede is a teenager from Nigeria, Africa. She is an award winning poet and the author of three published books. Her first book is titled *Lessons for Grandma*, her second book is titled *I Love to Go to School* and her debut novella is titled *Ladder To The Top*, all books available on online stores.

Elizabeth has contributed to several international literary anthologies. Her works have been published in online literary magazines and journals.

Her first book titled *Lessons from Grandma* was approved by Ondo State's Ministry of Education in Nigeria for 7th graders in Ondo State's secondary schools for the 2021-2023 academic sessions.

Elizabeth loves fictional works and poetry.

Wolf S. Helms

Wolf S. Helms is a cynical, scientific, irreverent person, taking pleasure in questioning set principles on scientific, moral, political and other grounds with a higher tendency towards those of science. He is from a rural section of the East Tennessee Valley.

Phoebe Humpton

Phoebe Humpton is a teen writer. Her writing is mostly YA fiction but she likes experimenting in different genres. She enjoys anything creative whether its writing, photography, or art.

Kenning Spath

Kenning Spath is a senior in high school. He currently resides in Henderson, Nevada and has lived there all his life. In his free time, when not applying to colleges and doing homework, Kenning loves to write poems and short stories.

Priscilla David

Priscilla O. David, is a poet and writer. She is a high school student in Nigeria who aspires to become a well-known writer and a renowned criminologist. She love reading and is a first time writer. She prays you love her writing.

Ainslee Davenport

Ainslee Davenport is a writer of fiction. Ainslee has been writing stories since kindergarten and has always been an avid reader. While Ainslee has lived many exciting and adventurous lives vicariously through fictional characters, she spends her time being a homebody in her hometown in Tennessee.

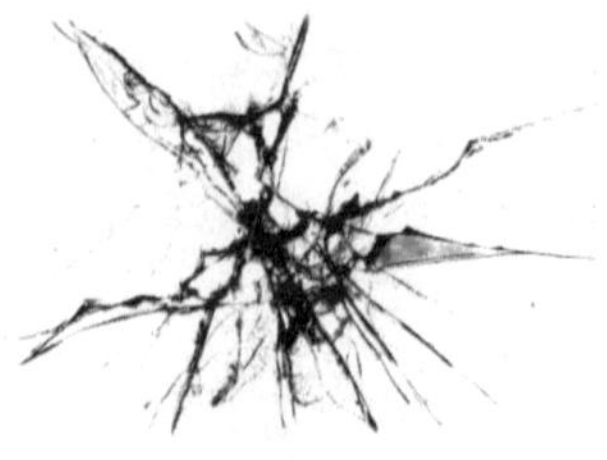

To find other literary anthologies, poetry, and novels published by Wild Ink Publishing LLC, please go to:

wild-ink-publishing.com